# CLAIM OF EON

## EON WARRIORS #6

## ANNA HACKETT

Claim of Eon

Published by Anna Hackett

Copyright 2020 by Anna Hackett

Cover by Melody Simmons of BookCoversCre8tive

Edits by Tanya Saari

ISBN (ebook): 978-1-922414-06-9

ISBN (paperback): 978-1-922414-07-6

**The Phoenix Adventures – SFR Galaxy Award Winner for Most Fun New Series and "Why Isn't This a Movie?" Series**

**Beneath a Trojan Moon – SFR Galaxy Award Winner and RWAus Ella Award Winner**

**Hell Squad – SFR Galaxy Award for best Post-Apocalypse for Readers who don't like Post-Apocalypse**

"Like Indiana Jones meets Star Wars. A treasure hunt with a steamy romance." – SFF Dragon, review of *Among Galactic Ruins*

"Strap in, enjoy the heat of romance and the daring of this group of space travellers!" – Di, Top 500 Amazon Reviewer, review of *At Star's End*

"Action, danger, aliens, romance – yup, it's another great book from Anna Hackett!" – Book Gannet Reviews, review of *Hell Squad: Marcus*

**Sign up for my VIP mailing list and get your *free box set* containing three action-packed romances.**

**Visit here to get started:** www.annahackett.com

# CHAPTER ONE

There was nothing like the feeling of standing on the bridge of a powerful warship and knowing you were in charge.

"Trennin, report," Second Commander Airen Kann-Felis said.

"All scans are clear, Second Commander," the warrior replied.

Airen stood facing the viewscreen—the familiar, never-ending view of space ahead of her. Behind her lay the tiered bridge she knew so well, full of black-clad Eon warriors at their stations. Her war commander, Malax Dann-Jad, was dealing with diplomatic issues in his office, leaving her in command.

No doubt his new Terran mate, Wren, was with him.

Airen had walked in on the pair kissing, and more, once or twice. She'd learned to knock very loudly. It was impossible to miss the depths of Malax's love and bond with Wren Traynor. It was a true bonding—one where his helian symbiont accepted his new mate as well. Airen

1

touched the band around her wrist that housed her own symbiont and felt a pulse of warmth.

She had no interest in a man, mating, or bonding of any sort. She'd attempted a few relationships in the past. Her stomach churned. She'd learned very quickly it wasn't for her. She was dedicated to her career, one in which there were very few female warriors. Her work required all her attention.

Her helian pulsed again. One day, she wanted to command her own warship. She wouldn't allow anything or anyone to interfere with that.

Although, for one fleeting second, she imagined what it would be like to have someone. Someone she trusted soul-deep.

When her belly churned again, she turned her attention back to the viewscreen.

There was a small flash of light on the screen, followed by several more. Frowning, she watched as several small, ragtag starships appeared out of nowhere.

"Second Commander," a warrior said, voice urgent. "Five intercepts in range and closing in on the *Rengard*."

Airen straightened, and studied the ships and their formation.

"Who the hell is that?" a deep voice said from behind her.

That deep, liquid voice shivered through her, and as always, she hid her violent reaction. It belonged to Sub-Captain Donovan Lennox of Earth's Space Corps.

He was one of their new Terran shipmates. Since the Traynor sisters had crashed into the Eon, attempting to get help for their planet, everything had changed. A long time ago, the Eon Empire had attempted first contact with the Terrans, but found them unruly and chaotic. Now, they had a shared enemy, and with several warriors happily mated to Terrans, the Eon Empire and Earth had a budding alliance.

That alliance included mixing their crews. Several warriors were now aboard Terran ships, and some Terrans from Space Corps were now on Eon warships.

That included this man she found very hard to ignore.

Donovan stepped up beside her, gaze on the screen. He was taller than her, with a muscular body, dark skin, and black hair he kept cut very short. Eon warriors wore their hair long, so the shorter hair was fascinating. His skin was also so much darker than the other Terrans she'd met, and she often caught herself admiring it.

His eyes were a light brown, and he smelled...very good. By the warriors, she sometimes wished she didn't have her helian-enhanced senses.

Airen's hands curled into fists, a clawing need flooding her belly. *No.* She'd felt desire before, or at least she thought she had. Something about Donovan Lennox ignited a wild hunger she'd never, ever experienced before.

Clearing her throat, she tried not to think about the fact that they'd kissed each other senseless in a maintenance conduit a week ago. She'd told him then that it had been an error in judgment. She didn't make mistakes. She'd fought hard for everything in her life, especially her career. She would not risk it for a moment of fleeting pleasure.

Since then, Donovan had listened to her. He'd been polite, competent. The perfect colleague.

She hunched her shoulders. Apparently, she was easily dismissed. She wasn't surprised. She'd had it happen before.

"Space pirates." She focused on the task at hand. "They are usually poorly organized, but sneaky."

Alarms sounded around the bridge.

"Their weapons are hot," a warrior called out.

"Sabin?" Airen said. "Fire a warning shot."

"I'm readying the laser array," Security Commander Sabin Solann-Ath replied.

A second later, the *Rengard* rumbled quietly beneath her feet, and then the laser array fired.

The pirate ships scattered.

The *Rengard* was currently patrolling the edge of Eon space, monitoring for Kantos activity. Their shared enemy—a ravenous, destructive, insectoid species intent on invading Earth and causing problems for the Eon— had been suspiciously quiet of late.

The *Rengard* had recently helped to rescue an Eon Medical Commander and a Terran space marine who'd been on a mission to save stolen helians from the Kantos. Airen kept her expression unchanged, but inside, she felt renewed horror at knowing the Kantos were trying desperately to find a way to disrupt an Eon warrior's bond with their helian.

She'd been bonded with her helian as a child, and couldn't imagine life without it. Helians gave warriors the ability to form armor and weapons at will, enhanced their bodies, healed their injuries. Her helian had been the only living thing she'd ever been able to depend on.

Medical Commander Aydin Kann-Ath from the *Desteron* and Lieutenant Jamie Park had barely survived with their lives, but they had recovered the helians the Kantos had stolen. And they'd fallen in love and ended up mated.

"Look," Donovan said with a frown. "One of the smaller ships has broken away from the group. Port side. He's getting too close."

*Get your focus back on the problem in front of you, Airen.* "Sabin."

"I see it." Sabin spun and barked orders to his security team.

"Security Commander!" another warrior cried. "Someone's attempting to hack the *Rengard's* systems."

*Cren.* "Block them!" Airen yelled.

Pirates were not known for their high-tech abilities. Her muscles tensed. The *Rengard* had a lot of experimental helian technology built into the ship, including a new high-tech and top-secret cloaking ability. They couldn't afford for anyone to get data on it.

"Do pirates usually take on warships?" Donovan asked.

She glanced his way. "No. They usually pick on easy prey."

"So this isn't usual behavior?"

"No." She pivoted. "Dayne, make sure—"

"They got in, Second Commander!"

Airen raced over to an empty comm station. "Get them out!"

"I'm trying," the young warrior said. "This is...not like *any* system attack I've seen before."

"They're copying data," Sabin growled.

"Sassy," Airen barked.

A second later, a confident female voice came out of the comp station. "You rang, Second Commander?"

"Pirates have accessed our system."

"What?" Sassy squawked.

Sassy was a helian that was bonded with some Terran technology, creating a sentient semi-artificial intelligence. One that had a unique personality all of her own.

"There!" Sassy cried seconds later. "I managed to push them out."

On-screen, the pirate ships started to retreat. Airen released the breath she was holding.

"Bring us around," Donovan said. "Go after the main ship. That'll stop whoever's giving them orders."

It was a good idea. Airen nodded. "Do it."

A second later, Sabin bombarded the main pirate ship with laser fire. One hit to their engines and the ship exploded.

"Second Commander," Sassy drawled. "I'm sorry to say this, but the pirates got some data. Several quads of data. It looks like it's a portion of our information on helian research."

*Cren.* This was a disaster. Airen met Donovan's gold-brown gaze. They both knew this was no simple pirate attack.

"Take them out," Airen ordered.

There were several barrages of laser fire from the *Rengard.* More ships disintegrated.

But one small ship raced toward the nearby planet.

"The data is on that ship," Sassy said.

"*Cren*," Sabin bit out. "The ship's out of range and in the planet's atmosphere."

Airen straightened. They couldn't let the pirates get away with the data.

"Let me update Malax, then I'm going down. Sabin, you're with me. Bring one of your security team."

The security commander nodded.

Donovan grabbed her arm and she felt the zing all the way to her shoulder. "I'm coming, too."

---

DONOVAN LENNOX PULLED his laser rifle out, checked it, then slung it over his shoulder. Next, he slid his laser pistol into the holster attached to his thigh. He was currently decked out in Space Corps' most high-tech, black-and-white spacesuit.

"All right, let's move," Airen called out.

He turned. *Damn.* Looking at Airen Kann-Felis was never a hardship, but covered in her black-scale, helian armor, with her brown hair in a neat braid, looking ready to take down any badass stupid enough to get in her way, made his pulse kick up a notch. Or three.

She had the most incredible eyes. Like all Eon warriors, they were black, with strands of color through them. Her strands were green—a pale turquoise color.

Sabin Solann-Ath, and a huge warrior called Matton, followed her into the shuttle hangar. Donovan brought up the rear.

He'd been aboard the *Rengard* for almost two weeks. The Eon warship was the best ship he'd ever seen, although he missed his small, scrappy ship. The *Divergent* was full of experimental tech, and the pride of the Space Corps fleet.

Still, as much as he missed his ship, his crew, and his captain and friend, Allie Borden, he was learning a lot from the Eon warriors.

And any time spent around Airen was time he enjoyed.

He'd kissed her, and it had been a hell of a kiss, but she'd shut him down. Still, he liked the way she watched him when she thought he wasn't looking.

Something told him that not many men got under that armor of hers—and he didn't mean the black scales of her helian armor.

He knew she had reservations about tangling with someone she worked with, but he reported directly to Malax, and he wouldn't be on the *Rengard* forever. They didn't have much time to explore this thing between them.

Donovan liked women, but not for the long term. He liked their sweetness, their softness, their smiles and sighs. But everything he'd learned about love meant he'd go nowhere near it. Ever. For his sake, and for the woman's.

He boarded the sleek Eon shuttle. Sabin dropped into the pilot seat, and as soon as Donovan and the others were harnessed up, the security commander wasted no time getting them off-ship. Moments later, they zoomed off the *Rengard*.

Donovan leaned back in his seat, enjoying the acceleration. He'd been born for space. He'd known that as a little boy, with a collection of starships he'd made himself from anything he could scavenge.

"Right." Airen turned in her seat. There was nothing soft about her right now; she was all warrior.

And damn if that didn't make him want her even more. *Shut it down, Lennox.*

He suspected if Airen knew his dirty thoughts, she'd skewer him with the sword her helian could make with a simple thought.

"This planet is uninhabited by sentient life forms, but watch out for the local flora and fauna. It's a jungle world, with unpredictable weather, but none of us will have any problem breathing, so we won't need contained oxygen. We'll track the pirate, recover the stolen data, and leave."

Donovan nodded. Simple.

It wasn't long before they hit atmo and the shuttle vibrated. As they descended, he peered through the viewscreen and saw huge thunderclouds in the distance. Below them lay dense vegetation—in a wild mix of green and yellow.

They landed in a tight clearing, leaves and branches hitting the sides of the Eon shuttle.

Matton opened the side door, and a second later, they all stepped outside. A wall of humidity hit them.

It smacked into Donovan's face like a heavyweight boxer's uppercut. *Great.* He was born and raised in Chicago, and had spent his career aboard starships with regulated environmental systems. He *hated* humidity.

"The pirates landed close to here, to the northeast," Sabin said. "Based on that location, we should split up and come in from either side. Matton and I will head north."

Airen hesitated for a second. "Fine, Donovan and I will veer east."

"Good hunting," Sabin said.

Donovan and Airen broke into a jog, slapping at leaves and vines as they moved through the vegetation.

"Warn me if you can't keep up," she said.

He stared at the back of her head. "I'll keep up."

She set a tough pace, but it was nothing he couldn't handle. They moved through a dense patch of yellow trees when Donovan spotted something. "Wait."

He crouched. He saw the edge of what he thought was a footprint in the damp dirt. It was faint.

Airen studied it. "It could have come from a boot."

He moved in a tight circle, spiraling outward while staring at the ground. A second later, he spotted another footprint. This one was deeper and clearer.

"Good spotting." There was admiration in her voice. "That's definitely a boot print."

"I'm a decent tracker." He glanced around, and spotted another footprint and some broken vines. "This way."

They moved together. God, she moved well—fluid and in total control. He could look at her all day.

They hadn't gone much farther when the rain hit. It started as a few big, fat droplets.

"*Cren*," she muttered.

Yeah, they'd lose the footprints.

The heavens opened. In seconds, they were drenched. It was raining so hard that it was hard to see.

They pushed on. "Careful." Donovan felt a tingle along his senses. "The asshole's close."

Her brow creased. "How do you know?"

"I feel it."

"Feel it?" Her frown deepened.

Suddenly, there was movement behind her. Something launched at Airen out of the vines.

Donovan tackled her and they hit the mud hard. She grunted under his weight.

"Up," she growled. "I can't fight on my back."

Donovan swiveled. It wasn't a pirate. It was some sort of animal.

Rising, he noted that the creature was vaguely humanoid, but much shorter than them. Its body was covered in pale fur, and its large eyes were a blue-green color. It vaguely reminded him of a large, muscular monkey. It also had claws. Long ones.

It hissed at them.

Donovan pulled out his laser pistol. There was a flash of green from beside him and he glanced over to see Airen had formed a sword on her arm. It was long and wicked, and glowing with a faint green color.

Damn, having a helian would be pretty fucking awesome.

Still, sometimes a simple laser pistol did the trick. He fired several times, clipping the animal's arm. The creature bolted into the leaves.

"I like the sword," he said.

"Thanks." She watched the vines, and when the creature didn't reappear, her sword dissolved away. She pushed strands of her sodden hair out of her face. "I think—"

All of a sudden, a body dropped out of the tree above them and slammed into her.

"Airen!" Donovan yelled.

# CHAPTER TWO

She hated sneaky pirates.

Despite the rain in her eyes, Airen shoved the foul-smelling man off her.

He leaped to his feet and spun, flashed metal teeth at her, then attacked. The jagged knife in his hand glinted dully in the gray light.

The idiot thought she was the softer target.

*Time to learn a lesson, my friend.*

Airen always tried to exude calm and control, but she had a temper. She kept it strictly locked away, most of the time.

Now, she let her anger punch through her and she formed a short sword. She blocked the pirate's hit. They traded several blows, slipping in the mud. The man was stronger than he looked.

When the pirate stumbled, she glanced sideways at Donovan. He held his laser pistol aimed and ready, but hadn't moved.

"Are you going to assist?" she asked.

"Nope."

She blinked. "Why not?"

"Because you've got it handled."

Airen stilled. She'd spent her entire career fighting for her spot, not letting big, strong warriors rush in to rescue her.

"Besides," he continued. "I really like watching you fight."

She heard the blatant appreciation in his deep voice, and felt it in places she'd never, ever admit to.

The pirate rushed at her again. She slammed him down and skewered his shoulder with her sword. He howled.

Donovan crouched and jammed his pistol against the man's cheek. "Don't move, or she's going to hurt you." Donovan patted the man's malodorous, scruffy clothes down. He found the data chip and held it up.

Airen took it, and her helian connected with the device, confirming that the *Rengard* data was on it.

"Why did you hack our system?" she asked. "Why did you steal this information?"

The pirate turned his head and spat on the ground.

Donovan shoved the pistol against the man's cheek even harder. "Answer, or I'll let her gut you."

The dark menace got through.

The pirate glanced between the two of them, then sucked in a breath. "We were hired. The Kantos have got a big, fat hard-on for the Eon and Terrans." His metal teeth flashed. "I'd watch your backs, if I were you. Those insects will be chewing on you before you know it. They have plans."

Donovan rose. "What plans?"

The pirate shrugged. "I don't know. They didn't tell me everything."

Donovan glanced at Airen. "What will we do with him?"

She wiped the water off her face. "Let him go. He can take his chances with the jungle."

The pirate didn't need to be told twice. He scrambled onto his hands and knees, slipped in the mud, then disappeared into the vegetation.

"Let's get out of this *cren*-cursed rain," she suggested.

"Hell, yeah, I'm with you on that."

They headed back toward the ship and Airen activated her comm. "Sabin? Come in."

"Airen?" Sabin's voice came through her communication device. "Did you find the pirate?"

"Yes. We have the data."

"Great, let's get off this cursed planet. We'll meet you at the ship."

"Acknowledged."

Even in the slick terrain, she admired Donovan's loose-hipped stride. She felt a flush of heat over her skin and sucked in a breath. *Cren*, this restless need to touch him was driving her crazy. She *would* control it.

At that moment, her boots slipped in the muck. He caught her arm, swinging her toward him, and her body slammed into his, her front plastered to his chest. She looked up, their faces close.

For several heartbeats, they both simply breathed. Airen's pulse pounded in her ears.

"I like watching you work, Airen," he said softly, breaking the silence.

Right now, his eyes looked gold. She'd noticed that before—they were normally pale brown, but they shifted to gold when he was really focused on something.

He was temptation—pure and powerful.

He didn't close the gap between them, even though heated tension sang in the air. She realized he wouldn't. She'd asked him to back off, and it appeared that Donovan Lennox was a man of his word.

She looked at him. "We should go."

He nodded and stepped back.

Airen felt a sense of loss and mentally cursed herself. She didn't need this. She couldn't afford to get tangled up with this man.

Suddenly, the mud beneath them began to boil. *By Ston's sword.*

"What the fuck?" Donovan muttered.

They both moved closer together, just as several tree roots speared up through the wet ground.

One root wrapped around Airen's leg, yanking her off her feet. Another one rushed up, curling around Donovan's waist.

Airen hit the ground, mud spraying her face. *Cren.* As she was dragged around the muddy ground, she formed a sword. She slashed at the root and freed herself. Leaping to her feet, she spat mud out of her mouth and spun. Donovan was cursing, his tree root lifting him off the ground. It tossed him from side to side.

"I thought there was nothing dangerous down here," he bellowed. He thumped a fist against the root.

"No sentient life forms." She strode toward him, dodging new roots as they broke out of the mud. "Apparently, there's some dangerous flora."

"You don't say."

Airen leaped up and swung her sword. It sliced through the root, freeing him. Another root whipped through the air and slammed into her. The force of the blow threw her against Donovan and they both crashed to the ground. She landed on top of him and heard him grunt.

"All right?" she asked.

"Yeah. You?"

Nodding, she sat up, shoving her saturated hair off her face. "Let's get—"

A long, thin tree root cleared the mud and arrowed at her. Before she could dodge, it wrapped around her neck.

*Cren.* Airen grabbed the root, trying to yank it off. It tightened, cutting off her air.

"Shit." Donovan knelt in front of her, his bigger hands closing over hers. He tugged hard, cursing steadily. "Come on, Second Commander. Use all that strength of yours." His voice was strained as he tried to pull the root off her.

She coughed and felt the burn in her lungs. Her helian was trying desperately to compensate for the lack of oxygen. Her vision blurred.

"Hey," Donovan snapped. "Look at me."

She stared into his face. He had a strong jaw and those eyes that reminded her of ancient Eon coins.

"Stay with me, Airen."

She sensed him doing something. Then she saw the knife in his hand, made of solid Terran steel.

A second later, the tree root was gone.

Airen sucked in a loud breath and toppled forward. He caught her against his chest.

"You're okay. Fuck." He ran a hand up and down her back.

She pulled in another long breath, her helian already stabilizing her body. "I'm fine."

Big hands cupped her cheeks. "You sure?"

She nodded. The rain was falling steadily, they were splattered with mud, and she saw the lines of worry etched into his strong face. Worry for her.

Airen didn't let herself think or question. She just closed the gap between them and kissed him.

For a humming second, Donovan didn't move, then his lips opened and he took her mouth.

Oh. *Oh.* He tasted like strength and frustrated desire. Like hot secrets and forbidden hunger. Like a shot of the Terran liquor she'd tried once, that had burned so smoothly down her throat.

His tongue stroked hers and she moaned, gripping his shoulders and pressing closer.

One of his hands slid around, cupping her head, holding her still as the kiss turned flaming hot and greedy. He made a low growl and it shivered through her, arrowing straight between her legs where she was already wet and needy.

"Damn, you taste good," he murmured against her mouth.

She tugged him closer and kissed him again.

"Airen? Airen?"

It took her a second to realize that it was Sabin's voice on her comm line.

She pulled back, even as a part of her wept in denial. She licked her lips, feeling so aroused and more than a little shocked at her behavior.

"I'm here, Sabin."

"Matton and I had to detour around a small ravine. Might take us a little longer to return to the ship."

"Acknowledged. Um, Donovan and I are still en route."

"See you soon."

Rising, Airen set her shoulders back. "We need to keep moving."

Donovan watched her, not saying anything.

She didn't know what she was feeling, so many different emotions churning inside her. "I'm sorry about the kiss."

"I'm not."

She closed her eyes. "Donovan—"

"Come on, Second Commander, let's get out of this rain."

They moved quickly through the jungle. It wasn't long before they spotted the shuttle.

They climbed aboard, and a few minutes later, Sabin and Matton arrived, equally sodden. Thankfully, it was time to leave the jungle behind.

Airen sat beside Sabin in the cockpit. Matton and Donovan strapped in behind them. She hoped the all-too-preceptive security commander didn't pick up her mood.

Outside, she tried for calm. Inside, she just wanted to crawl into Donovan's lap and devour him.

*By Alqin's axe.* She sucked in some breaths, watching as Sabin started the shuttle's engines and got them airborne.

As their shuttle broke the atmosphere, Matton grumbled, "I need a hot shower." Sabin made a wordless sound of agreement.

"Were you able to learn anything else?" Sabin asked, glancing first back at Donovan, and then at Airen.

Airen held up the data chip. "The pirate said the Kantos hired them."

Sabin cursed, his hands moving over the ship's controls. "I guessed as much. What have those fuckers got planned now?"

"Picking up some Terran curse words?" Donovan called out with a brief chuckle.

"Fuck, yeah."

Airen stared at the chip, worry eating at her. "The pirate alluded to the Kantos having attack plans, although he didn't have any more information."

Sabin glanced at her, the purple threads in his eyes glowing. "Well, we knew they weren't going to go away."

"No, they aren't," Airen agreed, swiping a droplet of water from her cheek.

"Here." Donovan leaned between the seats and held out an absorbent towel to her.

"Thanks." She wiped off her hair and face, turning to glance back at him.

She watched him dry himself off with a flex of

muscular arms and felt a rush of traitorous heat. Her hands clenched on her towel.

He caught her looking at him and smiled. The man had a gorgeous smile.

"*Rengard* ahead," Sabin called out.

*Work.* That's what she needed right now. Her reason for everything.

She turned to face her warship through the viewscreen, but thoughts of the distracting Terran that made her want to crawl out of her skin were still in her head.

---

WHEN DONOVAN HAD FINISHED his shift for the day, he headed to the *Rengard* gym. He was wearing black shorts, a tight, black compression shirt, and his favorite battered Nikes.

As he entered the gym, he called out to the warriors who were training on the mats, and then hit the treadmill.

Like all Eon technology, it was kick ass.

Just like a certain warrior he knew.

He hadn't seen Airen since they'd returned yesterday from the jungle planet and she'd gone to the tech team to get the chip analyzed. He couldn't prove it, but he suspected the second commander was avoiding him.

The kiss had left her rattled. She'd just about blown his head off with that kiss. His lips curved. God, he could still taste her, hear the husky little noises she'd made.

His roster today had included a stint with the ship's

navigators. Thankfully, the work had kept him busy and occupied until now. He ran until he was sweaty. The training warriors left, calling out goodbyes. Moments later, the doors opened again, and Airen entered wearing workout gear.

*Damn.*

His cock throbbed, letting him know just how much it appreciated seeing the second commander. She wore tight leggings, and a thin top that clung to her. Her clothing was all black and he wondered if she ever wore color. She'd look stunning in red, or turquoise.

She spotted him, hesitated, then nodded.

Donovan liked knowing he upset the steady second commander's equilibrium. He wouldn't be on the *Rengard* forever. And while he didn't believe in love and long-term, he fully believed in short-term and mutually satisfying.

When he finished on the treadmill, he moved onto the mat and started stretching. "Hi, Airen."

"Donovan."

"Any news about the data on the chip?" he asked.

She nodded. "We recovered all of the stolen data." She stretched her slender arms above her head and he forced himself not to look at her perfect breasts—he'd already noted that they were high, not large, not small. *Perfect.*

"But there's other data on the chip, as well," she added.

He straightened. "Really?"

"It's encrypted." Her nose wrinkled. "Some sort of

chaotic encryption the pirates have used. The team's working on it with Wren and Sassy."

"Could have helpful information on there," he mused.

"Or it could just be space pirate crap."

She moved to the wall of weapons and picked a sword off the rack. Back on the mat, she started swinging the weapon and moving through a routine full of kicks and lunges. Damn, his mouth went dry as he watched her bend and then slash with that sword out.

She was beautiful. He was attracted to that, sure, but he also liked her quiet strength, not to mention the softness she tried to hide. Donovan had grown up with a houseful of sisters, so he knew how to read a woman, especially when she was trying to hide something.

Airen paused. "Would you like me to show you some moves?"

"Sure."

He picked a larger sword off the wall—longer, a little sturdier.

"Okay, hold it like this." She demonstrated. "Now follow my moves."

He watched her carefully, and soon he was mimicking the movements, a new sheen of perspiration on his face.

They moved in tandem, swinging and slashing.

"You're a quick learner," she said.

"Always have been. When I was younger, I had to be."

She raised a brow.

"My dad left when I was young. My mom ended up being a single mother with four kids to provide for."

"You have three siblings."

*Was that a faint, wistful note in her voice?* "Three older, nosy, know-it-all sisters. They like thinking they can boss me around." He grinned. Damn, he missed them all. "I had to join Space Corps to escape them."

A small smile tipped Airen's lips.

"You have siblings, family?"

"No." She turned away, snatched up a cleaning rag and started running it over the sword. She returned the weapon to the wall.

Frowning, Donovan followed her. "I'm sorry." He touched her arm. "I didn't mean to make you sad."

"I'm not." The words came out fast, and then she sighed. "Old news. I was found as an abandoned infant, and raised as a ward of the Empire."

His frown deepened. So, she'd been alone right from a baby? "I thought having babies wasn't exactly easy for the Eon? If it requires medical intervention, wouldn't there be a record of your birth?"

Her mouth flattened. "There was no record. I was just unwanted."

"Hey." He pulled her closer and then wrapped his arms around her.

She stiffened.

"It's just a hug, Airen. For comfort."

"That's not required, Donovan. I've comforted myself my entire life, and like I said, this is old news."

"Yeah, but I need the comfort. I hate to think of you being so young and alone."

Slowly, she relaxed against him. "It wasn't all bad. I was well-cared for and entered the Warrior Academy as soon as I could. It taught me to be self-sufficient and independent."

He wondered who'd hugged her or taught her about boys or been proud of her achievements.

Then the gym doors opened and she jerked away like he was on fire.

Two young warrior recruits entered and nodded at them. "Second Commander. Sub-Captain."

Airen nodded back.

Once the recruits were busy on the equipment on the other side of the gym, Donovan studied her. "You aren't allowed to be off-duty?"

"A second commander is always on duty. And doesn't get caught hugging crewmates in the gym."

"You're allowed to have a life, Airen. Even your war commander is mated now."

"That's different."

"Because you're a woman?"

"Partly. There aren't many female warriors, so we always have to work hard for our place. But mostly because I had to fight to become a warrior. I had no family, no connections. Everything I have, I earned myself." She released a breath. "And I almost jeopardized it fraternizing with another warrior once. I won't make that mistake again."

Donovan felt a burn of anger. Some asshole had betrayed her trust? "Someone hurt you."

"No, he just opened my eyes."

"Who is he? I'll—"

25

That earned him a faint smile. She touched his arm. "Do you think I need defending?"

"No, you can defend yourself, but that doesn't mean I can't help."

"He isn't on the *Rengard*. And it's just another old fact." Her hand stroked down his arm, and he wasn't even sure she realized she'd done it.

Then he saw the way she was staring at his chest.

"You feel it," he murmured. "The pull."

She dropped her hand, her fingers curling. "I'd be lying if I said no."

"I want to kiss you. Badly. I want you to touch me."

Color appeared in her pale cheeks and she squeezed her eyes closed for a second. "Neither of us want or need this. It'll be a huge distraction and cause problems."

"You don't know that."

"I do," she said firmly.

"I want to pull you down on these mats and tear your clothes off."

Her breath hitched. "That might be more than those warriors expected to see in the gym." Her lips firmed. "You can't say things like that, Donovan."

He blew out a breath. "Okay, okay. We'll be friends."

"Friends. I'd like that." Gorgeous black eyes streaked with green met his. "But I'm not sure I can do it."

"What?" he said. "Why? You can trust me, Airen—"

She held up a slim hand. "I know. I haven't known you long, but it's been long enough to see that you're a man of honor."

"So?"

She leaned down and grabbed her gear, slinging her

26

bag on her shoulder. She stepped closer to him. "I'm not sure I can stop myself from dragging *you* down to the floor and tearing *your* clothes off."

Donovan's gut filled with flames and he groaned. "Airen, you can't say stuff like that and not expect me to act on it."

"Don't worry, I'm very good at controlling my desire for things I can't have. Good night, Donovan."

She strode out, leaving him with a hard cock, and a fierce need to carry her straight to his bed and make her beg for him to do delicious things to her.

# CHAPTER THREE

O n the bridge, Airen stood at a large light table with Malax and Wren.

"I've managed to crack some of the encryption." The Terran woman was small and curvy, with curly, brown hair. She pushed at an errant curl, frustration evident on her face. "But this stuff is crazy. There's no rhyme or reason or rhythm."

Malax touched his mate's back. Wren leaned into him, relaxing a little.

The pair was so connected. Airen could practically touch their bond. She looked at the light table, instead of at the couple. Even though she knew she didn't want that, she wondered what it'd be like to have one person become the center of her universe. Someone who she could depend on, and who would always be there to support her.

She shook her head. Her career was the center of her universe.

"These look like coordinates," Airen said.

Malax nodded. "We have some pirate maps in the database. Let's see if anything matches up."

"I'm already one step ahead of you, and I'm a *genius*." Sassy's voice came through loud and clear, and she sounded pleased with herself. "I've already matched some locations."

Wren smiled and Malax shook his head.

"Let's see," the war commander said.

Maps flashed up on the light table, with several locations marked by glowing gold dots.

Malax frowned, pressing a hand to the table as he leaned forward. "Those are Eon outposts."

"Correct," Sassy said. "One is a colony, and the other four are science outposts. They're all close to the edge of Eon space."

Airen tapped her fingers against her leg. "Why do the pirates have all these marked?"

No one had the answer, but Wren looked worried, and Malax looked angry.

Her war commander swiveled. "Airen, contact these outposts and have them raise their alert levels."

"Yes, War Commander."

"Sassy, keep working on decoding the rest of the pirate data with Wren."

"We're already on it, big guy," the AI replied.

Wren and Malax left, but Airen remained, staring at the table. Sabin moved in beside her.

"I don't like this," the security commander said.

"I don't, either. This has Kantos treachery written all over it."

"These are science outposts, so there is no heavy

warrior presence. We know the Kantos want to find a way to neutralize our helians."

And the aliens also wanted to find a way to utilize the helians' unique abilities for themselves. They'd already dabbled with fusing helians with their weaponry.

It was vital Airen's team decoded the rest of the information. She glanced around the bridge. "Is Donovan with you today?"

"No," Sabin replied. "He has a few assigned days with engineering and maintenance." Sabin paused. "He is extremely competent."

"You like him."

"I was sure an alliance with the Terrans was a mistake, but he's helping prove me wrong."

A warrior from Sabin's security team called out, and he moved away. Airen's portable comp pinged and she pulled the small screen out. She had a message.

*Donovan: Good morning, Second Commander.*

She touched the screen.

*Airen: Good morning, Sub-Captain. How's Engineering?*

*Donovan: Engineering is interesting. Although, your chief engineer doesn't like Terrans much.*

*Airen: Our Engineering Commander is still a little upset that Wren hijacked the* Rengard *and kept us hostage for a week.*

*Donovan: Uh-oh, you got me into trouble. I laughed and he skewered me with his grumpy gaze.*

Airen found herself smiling. It was getting harder to deny, but she liked this smart Terran.

*Donovan: I'm guessing you're on the bridge?*

*Airen: Yes.*

*Donovan: Bet you're standing in front of the viewscreen, feet hip-width apart, back straight, looking in-charge and badass.*

Airen shifted her feet. She was standing exactly like that.

*Airen: Actually, I'm lounging in my seat, studying rosters.*

*Donovan: Liar.*

She smiled. Then she glanced up and spotted a young warrior eyeing her curiously. Airen cleared her throat. Okay, so she didn't smile much on the bridge.

*Airen: My shift is almost over. I need to finish my work.*

*Donovan: Let me guess, you'll head to the gym and work out.*

*Cren*, he'd only been aboard the ship two weeks and had her worked out. Was she so predictable?

*Airen: Yes.*

*Donovan: I like you in your workout gear.*

She felt a flare of heat.

*Airen: Sub-Captain, time for you to get back to work.*

*Donovan: Yes, ma'am. You should try some music with your workout.*

*Airen: Music is a distraction.*

*Donovan: Distractions can be good, Airen. Have a good workout.*

There were no more messages. At the end of her shift, Airen checked in with Malax to see if Sassy and Wren had made more progress with the encryption.

"Nothing yet," he grumbled.

With a nod, Airen left. She stopped at her cabin to change her clothing, and spotted a box sitting on her bed.

*Who the* cren *had been in her quarters?*

She snatched it up and saw a note flutter to the ground. She lifted it.

*You'll like it, I promise — D.*

Her heart did a funny flutter. Donovan had left her a gift.

She opened the box and frowned at the small Terran device. She touched a button.

Donovan's voice came out of it. "I put some classics on here for you. Enjoy, Airen."

Ignoring the effect of his smooth, deep voice on her system, she listened as music started to play. It was a loud song with a pumping beat. She shook her head, but she did take it with her while she changed.

If she was tapping her foot by the end of the song, well, she wasn't admitting to it.

She grabbed her gym bag, hesitated, then placed the music player inside.

---

DONOVAN CRAWLED out of the maintenance conduit, lugging the heavy toolbox behind him.

Ahead, three Eon engineers were with him, checking systems panels. That included the Engineering Commander Narann-Jad.

Despite the fact that they were the *Rengard*'s engineers, they were still warriors—big and muscled. He had no doubt they could hold their own in a fight.

He felt a vibration in his pocket and pulled out his portable comp. He smiled. There was a message from Airen.

*Airen: Thank you for the music player.*

*Donovan: You like the music? Told you it would be good to work out with.*

*Airen: I don't listen to music when I work out.*

Donovan rolled his eyes and shook his head. She sure had a stubborn streak.

*Donovan: Are you lying to me, Second Commander?*

*Airen: Eon warriors do not lie.*

*Donovan: That isn't an answer. I thought you'd like this band. It's one of my favorites. You should listen to song ten. I marked it for you.*

*Airen: Perhaps when I have time.*

God, she got to him. He found himself grinning like a loon.

*Airen: How's Engineering?*

*Donovan: Reminded me why I scraped through my engineering classes at the Space Corps Academy.*

*Airen: You're an intelligent man. I find it hard to believe that you scraped through any class.*

*Donovan: You think I'm smart? Well, I aced those classes, but what I mean is that I scraped by because I was bored out of my brains during them. I'm a man of action.*

*Airen: I see.*

*Donovan: I promise you, I do not find these maintenance conduits interesting at all.*

*Airen: You're there to learn.*

*Donovan: I'd prefer to be watching you.*

*Airen: Stick to appropriate comments, Sub-Captain.*

He grinned. If he didn't know better, he'd say Airen was enjoying this.

*Donovan: As you wish, Second Commander.*

There was a pause and he thought she'd left him.

*Airen: Do you miss your ship? Your crew?*

*Donovan: Yes, but I'm learning a lot. I do miss my favorite drink. I'd give anything for a glass of cold cola.*

*Airen: Our synthesizers can make whatever you want.*

*Donovan: I tried. Doesn't taste the same.*

"Sub-Captain," one of the engineers called out. "You'll enjoy seeing these energy couplings."

Donovan swallowed a groan. "Great."

He tapped the screen again.

*Donovan: Duty calls.*

*Airen: Thanks again for the music.*

*Donovan: My pleasure.*

After he tucked his comp away, he focused on learning about the *Rengard's* high-tech innards. He had to admit that some of it was interesting. The way they'd incorporated their helian technology into the ship was fascinating. They hadn't shared much about the helian core that was a key part of the *Rengard's* systems, but what he had noted was impressive.

And at the same time, he thought he detected that grumpy Narann-Jad might be thawing toward him.

By the time his shift was over, Donovan was hungry, thirsty, and ready to relax. He had exited the lift and headed down the corridor to his cabin, when he almost ran into Wren.

"Hey, Wren."

"Donovan." Her smile was bright and wide. "How are things?"

"I've seen way more maintenance conduits than I wanted to."

Her nose wrinkled. "Dude, I spent a week playing hide-and-seek in those tunnels, with warriors trying to track me down."

He grinned. "You win. You shouldn't go around stealing warships from angry alien warriors, you know."

She rolled her eyes. "I'll keep that in mind."

"Any luck with the pirate data?"

Wren groaned. "Don't bring that up. Malax is grumpy as hell. Airen looked very unhappy, and I thought Sabin was ready to shoot lasers out of his eyes. Apart from those locations of the Eon outposts, nothing. The outposts have been warned to beef up the security, but who knows what the pirates and/or the Kantos have planned."

Donovan gripped her shoulder. "We won't let those insect bastards win."

"Right." She tilted her head. "You heading to your cabin?" She had a funny look on her face.

"Yes. Why?"

"Oh, nothing." She grinned. "Have a good night."

Donovan entered his cabin and scanned around. Nothing looked out of place.

Then he saw a card resting on the built-in desk beside the bed.

*Check your cooler.*

It wasn't signed. He strode over to the small refrigerator cooler and opened it. A bottle of dark liquid rested on the top shelf.

He pulled the bottle out and gave it a little shake, watching it fizz. He popped the top and took a sip.

Cool cola slid down his throat, and he groaned with pleasure.

It was perfect. Just like the real thing.

He grabbed his comp.

*Donovan: Know anything about the drink in my fridge?*

*Airen: I don't know why you like that brown liquid so much. It tastes foul. And it has no nutritional properties.*

*Donovan: It's an acquired taste. How did you get it right?*

*Airen: Wren helped.*

*Donovan: Thank you, Second Commander.*

*Airen: My pleasure. We want our Terran allies to feel comfortable aboard the* Rengard. *Have a good evening.*

Donovan sank down into his armchair, sipped his cola, and smiled. A certain tough, female warrior was starting to thaw a little, too.

# CHAPTER FOUR

The peal of the ship's emergency alarms had Airen leaping out of bed. She shoved her hair out of her eyes, quickly fighting off the grip of sleep.

By the time she was upright, her comm chimed. "Second Commander," a warrior's voice said. "Your presence is requested on the bridge."

"On my way."

It took a second to pull on her uniform and braid her hair. When she strode onto the bridge, a thunderous-looking Malax stood, staring at the viewscreen, flanked by Sabin and Donovan.

All the men had clenched jaws, and an upset Wren stood in front of Malax. He had his arms wrapped around his mate.

"What's happened?" Airen demanded.

Donovan turned and their gazes met. He'd clearly been dragged from his bed as well, as intriguing dark stubble covered his strong jaw. She made herself look at Malax. Right now, she couldn't afford any distractions.

"Pirates have attacked Thessa."

She sucked in a breath. Thessa was one of the Eon science outposts.

She turned to the viewscreen. On the feed, Eon were running in all directions, dodging explosions and screaming. The colony was being attacked and bombarded.

"There are four ships in orbit," Sabin said. "All space pirates."

"They're not using typical space pirate weaponry," Airen noted.

"No," Malax said. "This is Kantos weaponry."

"It's likely a trap," Donovan said. "To lure the *Rengard* to this outpost."

Airen nodded. "They still want something off our ship. Likely the helians, or at least another attempt at our helian research data."

"I know, but we will *not* abandon our people," Malax said.

"Forty ship minutes until we reach Thessa, War Commander," a warrior called out from his station.

It was a tense forty minutes. Airen tried not to fidget while she watched the fighting on the screen.

The security contingent of warriors at Thessa were fighting the pirate foot soldiers. Several buildings were destroyed and burning.

It was nighttime on the small moon. The pirates had attacked in the middle of the night, when people were sleeping, and at their most sluggish. Typical cowardly pirate tactics.

"You okay?" Donovan stepped up beside her.

"No," she answered. "But I will be, once I've taken a few pirates down." Hard and painfully.

"We'll make them pay." His voice vibrated with quiet conviction.

She nodded. "But how many will die? There are children at that outpost, Donovan."

He gripped her arm, squeezed. Such a small move, but strangely, it made her mind settle.

"We'll get there soon and do what needs to be done."

HE SQUEEZED HER ARM AGAIN, then he moved away.

A small comfort. She sucked in a breath. She hadn't lied to him when she said she hadn't had anyone to comfort her, ever. She'd been raised as a ward of the Empire, and the instructors at the Warrior Academy didn't hug the young recruits.

She touched the helian on her wrist and felt it pulse. It was the only thing she'd felt truly close to her entire life. She respected her fellow warriors, counted Malax as a friend, but she'd never go to him for personal advice or comfort.

Finally, Thessa appeared in range.

"On-screen," Malax called out.

Thessa was a small, forest moon, and the four pirate ships were clustered together in orbit.

"Take them out," he ordered.

"With pleasure," Sabin replied.

Missiles launched from the *Rengard*, arcing through

space. Impassively, Airen watched as the pirate ships turned to face them.

But it was too late. A few missiles were all it took.

The first ship blew into tiny pieces. The others tried to run, abandoning their people on the ground. *Typical.*

But Sabin and his team were ruthless. Moments later, all the ships were just space debris.

"Let's get to the surface," Malax commanded.

Airen saw one of Sabin's rare smiles. "I'll assemble my team."

Malax kissed Wren. "We'll be back soon."

"Be careful down there," the woman said.

When Airen entered the hangar bay with several of her warriors, she'd already formed her helian armor.

She spotted Donovan, suited up in his Terran space-suit. The high-tech fabric clung to him, highlighting every muscle in his body. He could pass for a warrior, except for the short hair and darker skin.

"Ready?" he asked.

"Oh, I'm past ready," she said.

They all settled in their seats aboard the shuttle and pulled their harnesses on. The shuttle took off, several others following behind them. Malax rose, standing behind Sabin's pilot seat. His gaze was on the viewscreen.

The small, green moon got larger, and then they were descending into the moon's atmosphere.

Plumes of smoke rose up in the early-morning darkness. As they neared the science outpost, there was a violent explosion on the ground.

*Cren.* Airen tried to calm her racing heartbeat. There

were children at this outpost, families and scientists. They weren't all warriors.

These pirates would pay. The Kantos would pay.

As soon as they landed on the outskirts of the community, every warrior on the shuttle stood.

Malax pressed the side door controls. "Let's save our people. Protect our Empire."

They poured out of the shuttle and broke into a run, moving in formation, weapons forming on their arms.

She glanced at Donovan. He held his rifle with total ease. It was clear he knew how to use it well.

The sharp scent of smoke filled her senses.

"Look out for traps," she warned Donovan. "The pirates are well known for that."

They sprinted through the trees, and Airen's senses sharpened. She was a warrior and she was ready to fight.

Ahead, the ground gave way in a few places. Several warriors fell into freshly dug holes that had been covered by leaves.

She heard cursing.

"Pull them out," Sabin ordered.

"There's some sort of chemical in the bottom," someone cried out. "It's burning!"

"Anyone hurt?" Malax boomed.

"No!"

*Cren-cursed pirates.* Airen watched Donovan's body tense. She scanned ahead. "What?"

Suddenly, he spun and jumped on her. They hit the ground, just as several projectiles whizzed over their heads.

"Down!" Malax roared. The war commander crouched behind a tree.

"You okay?" Donovan asked, moving off her.

She nodded, dusting herself off as they crouched.

"There." She spotted movement in the trees.

Donovan moved. *Fast.* He leaped up.

"Donovan!" she whisper-yelled.

He ran across the ground, his powerful body moving like liquid. Several projectiles peppered the ground behind him.

Heart pounding, Airen formed a blaster on her arm and shot a blast of energy into the trees. She heard a scream.

Donovan got closer, his weapon drawn. He fired up into the branches, then swiveled and fired again. He moved and squeezed off another shot, using his weapon like an extension of his body.

He disappeared into the trees. A second later, he strode out, dragging a writhing pirate behind him.

"Tie him up," Malax ordered. "Once we subdue the rest, we'll have a nice chat with our new friend."

The pirate was injured and bleeding, and Malax's tone made him blanch.

Another explosion rocked the outpost.

"Let's move!" Airen yelled.

---

DONOVAN USED HIS LASER SCOPE, zeroing in on a running pirate and fired.

The laser hit the man, and he stumbled and fell. The

Eon woman he'd been chasing flew into the arms of an Eon man, sobbing against his chest.

These Eon weren't warriors. They were scientists and their families.

A blast of energy filled the air, and he turned to see Airen firing on a trio of pirates. He didn't understand the intricacies of how the helians converted energy, but it was amazing to see the helian weapons at work.

Malax sprinted forward, Sabin one step behind him. Both men had formed swords on their arms. Malax's was a long, single blade that whistled through the air as he attacked.

His blade crashed into a pirate's curved sword, and the pirate went down under the powerful blows.

Sabin had a sword on each arm, both glowing a faint purple, whirling as he fought.

Damn, the man was fast. He was like a deadly whirlwind.

Airen leaped into the air, and her blaster morphed, changing into a sword.

*By God, she was something.*

She slammed into a group of pirates, swinging and slicing.

Donovan fired on several others, then spotted one pirate crouched by a building, doing something with his hands. He was close to Airen, but she had her back to him and was busy fighting. *What the hell was he up to?* Then the pirate turned and ran like the hounds of hell were nipping at his ankles.

Something was wrong.

"Airen!"

She couldn't hear him in the midst of the fight. Then he saw the flicker of flames in the building where the pirate had been. His gut went tight, his instincts screaming.

He broke into a sprint, his boots pounding on the ground. He picked Airen up, lifting her off her feet.

"What—?" She almost sliced him with her sword.

Then the building exploded.

The blast knocked Donovan off his feet. He slammed into the ground, covering Airen, as a fireball washed over them.

Suddenly, she sat up, slapping at his back. "You're on fire!"

"Suit will protect me." He did feel a few unwelcome twinges.

They both turned and saw the building where Airen had been standing was now a smoking ruin.

"Thanks," she said.

He nodded.

Screams pierced the night. Donovan tensed. Those were a child's screams.

He leaped up, scanning the ruined outpost. He spotted a child on the roof of a long, flat building. A pirate was chasing her.

"We need to get to her," he said.

"Wait," Airen said.

Several *Rengard* warriors joined them.

But Donovan only had eyes for the little girl. The way her dark hair flew behind her and her skirts moved around her little body reminded him of his sisters when they were kids. The pirate was gaining on her.

He took a step, but Airen grabbed his arm.

"Wait," she said again.

"There's no time," he barked.

She scowled at him. "It's a trap, Donovan. They'll be waiting for us. We need—"

"There's no damn time!"

The pirate snatched the girl off her feet and Donovan broke into a sprint.

"Donovan! I'm ordering you to wait."

"Screw that."

He pounded up the stairs attached to the building and then leaped onto the roof. He whipped his laser pistol out and fired.

The pirate collapsed and the girl screamed again.

"I've got you," he said.

The girl flung herself at him, pressing her face into his gut.

"Let's get you out of here. You're safe now."

There was movement on the roof. Three pirates rose from behind vent units. One was huge. Over seven feet tall. He lifted a massive axe high over his shoulder.

*Shit.*

Donovan backed up, and when the little girl stumbled, he lifted her up with his left arm.

With his right, he fired his gun.

"Keep your head down," he warned the girl. She nodded, and burrowed her face against his chest.

The big pirate advanced, slamming his axe down and roaring. The roof shook.

Donovan backed up. The pirates fired their weapons,

and he ducked down behind a vent unit, curling around the girl.

Laser fire tore into the unit, leaving burning holes in it. The girl screamed in terror.

The big pirate lumbered toward them.

*Shit.* They were pinned down, and the pirates were blocking the stairs. He was fucked.

All of a sudden, a slim body sailed over the edge of the roof.

Airen landed with a slight bend of her knees, right in front of the huge pirate.

"Now!" she yelled.

Several other Eon warriors leaped onto the roof, arms up, weapons morphing on their arms.

The warriors landed, lifted their weapons, and fired. Nets shot out, tangling around the pirates.

Airen held a thin line of metallic rope in her hands, spinning it so fast it was a blur.

The big pirate growled and swung out with his axe.

Donovan's mouth went dry, but Airen ducked the axe, pivoted and threw the rope.

It tangled around the giant's legs. He crashed down, and then Airen's weapon changed. She fired an electrical charge that hit the big pirate, causing him to shudder. The green electricity skated over him, and he collapsed.

Donovan released a breath.

Airen strode toward him and he rose, the little girl in his arms.

"Are you injured?" Airen's voice was cool, hard.

He shook his head.

"The girl?"

"She's fine, Airen. I—"

"Derril, take the girl and find her family."

As a warrior moved forward, Donovan stared at Airen. She was looking through him, not at him. Her anger was like a sharp blade that he could feel on his skin, her helian amplifying the sensation.

But as always, Airen was keeping it in check. All that cool control of hers.

The little girl patted his cheek, a silent thank you, then went with the warrior.

Donovan dragged in a breath. "Airen, I'm—"

"You didn't listen." Her voice was low and harsh. "You ignored my orders."

*Fuck.* He had. In the heat of battle, he was used to being creative. Allie had the same temperament as him. In fact, he was sometimes the more cautious of the two of them.

"I know. Seeing that girl in danger—"

"You've never fought space pirates." Her voice was like a whip. "We know their tactics. Ambushes are their favorite."

Donovan blew out a breath. She was right. She was pissed, and she had every right to be. "You're—"

"You're here to learn. You could've gotten yourself or the girl killed."

His own anger spiked. She wasn't letting him talk. "Or she might've been killed before you made it up here."

"Terrans are too impulsive."

He reached for her. "Now, wait a minute—"

She stepped back, avoiding his touch, and that made him angrier. He opened his mouth and realized her warriors were watching them. He'd already ignored her orders in front of them. Shit, he'd ignored her in front of her team.

He tried to calm his voice. "Airen—"

"We need to see to the injured." She turned away.

"We aren't finished talking about this," he said quietly.

She glanced back, a distant look in her eyes. That cut him.

"We are definitely finished, Sub-Captain."

# CHAPTER FIVE

Airen strode through the outpost, cataloging the work that had been done, and the jobs that still needed completing. The sun was rising, casting bright light on all the damage and destruction. Weary, shocked residents stood around, clinging to each other.

She passed the *Rengard* medical commander, Thane Kann-Eon. The tall man nodded at her. He and his team were treating some of the outpost residents who had been injured. Thane was one of the most respected doctors in the Eon fleet. A little older than her, he wore his hair shorter than most warriors. Silver dusted his temples, but his body was still muscled and powerful.

*Rengard* warriors had put out all the fires, helping the local warriors secure the damaged buildings. She spotted Donovan and her belly coiled, but she pulled in a breath and let ice fill her veins.

Her helian fought her, but she subdued the emotions. He'd ignored her order, on her mission, in front of her warriors. She turned away.

Malax stood in the center of the outpost, hands on his hips.

"Three dead, six injured," she said. "All the children are fine. It could've been far worse."

Malax made an angry sound. "The attack seems pointless. There's nothing missing. No purpose."

"Pirates are usually chaotic—"

"Pirates always calculate their profit." The gold strands in his eyes glowed. "What did this gain them?"

She blew out a breath. "I don't know."

Malax looked at her. "Are you all right?"

"Fine. A little tired." And a lot angry.

She checked in with the medical team, then talked with some of the local scientists. She walked to the edge of the outpost where it was clear the pirates had entered.

"Airen?"

Donovan's voice made her stiffen. "I'm busy, Sub-Captain."

As she turned away from him, he grabbed her arm. She tried to tug free, but the stubborn Terran held on.

"Look," he said. "I know you're angry with me."

"No, I'm *busy*."

"I'm sorry." He ran a hand over his hair. "I messed up."

She hadn't expected an apology. Still, it didn't change anything. "It's fine. Now, I need to get back to work."

He frowned. "Don't freeze me out, Airen. I made a mistake. I want to talk—"

"We talked, you apologized, we're done."

There was a flare in his gold-brown eyes. He leaned closer. "We are *not* done. Be angry. Yell at me."

"I do not yell, and I'm not angry."

"Yes, you are. Look, I'm used to working my own way with my crew. We're more impulsive and spontaneous, and I'm still adjusting—"

"Donovan, it's done."

He muttered a curse under his breath. "Right. You're busy erecting those walls again to keep me out because you're pissed."

"I'm *not* angry," she growled, her voice low. "I was starting to trust you, and you—"

His eyes softened. "Airen..."

"It's done. I know better." She tugged her arm free. She needed some space between them.

"I'm not him. Whoever the asshole is who didn't trust you, or your strength and skill. I messed up because I'm used to something different, not because I don't think you are fucking good at your job."

She just stared at him.

His face twisted. "Airen, dammit—"

There was a rustle in the trees beside them.

Airen turned her head and saw glowing, pinprick eyes through the leaves. Then there was the sound of a large body running through the trees.

Donovan yanked out his pistol. "Kantos!"

He launched into the forest, and Airen sprinted after him, forming her sword. "Donovan!"

They rushed through the trees and bushes, and a moment later, reached a clearing. The Kantos soldier rose to its full height on its four, jointed legs.

The alien held two razor-sharp arms up in front of a torso covered in thick, brown, armored plates. Its flat face was dominated by four beady, glowing, yellow eyes, and a narrow mouth filled with sharp teeth.

It swung an arm at Donovan, and he ducked and fired.

Airen knew those arms were sharp enough to slice him open. She lunged, her sword flashing in the early-morning light. It hit into the hard shell of the Kantos' torso.

The alien's eyes flashed and it made a buzzing noise. Then it spun and rushed at Airen.

The Kantos slammed into her, knocking her down.

A sharp arm descended and she rolled to the side. The Kantos hit the dirt.

There was more laser fire, then Donovan rammed into the Kantos, knocking it off her.

Airen leaped up at the same time Donovan did. The Kantos darted into the trees, moving quickly on those four long legs.

"Shit!" Donovan ran and she kept pace one step behind him.

She shoved branches aside, feeling them slap against her face. A moment later, they came out at the edge of a large flat area. The horrible smell of mud and decay slammed into her.

"Dammit," Donovan bit out. "A fucking swamp."

The muddy area stretched out ahead of them. Donovan stared after the Kantos as it leaped across rocks and small, high points of dirt dotting the swamp like tiny islands.

"For the first time ever, I wish I had four legs." Donovan jumped onto a large, flat rock, then another.

Dragging in a breath, Airen followed. There was no way they could move as fast as the Kantos soldier.

Still, they weren't giving up.

They leaped across the swamp. Ahead of her, Donovan's foot slipped and his leg sank into the swampy mud up to his knee.

"Ugh, this smells rank." He yanked on his leg, but it didn't move. "Crap, I'm stuck."

She landed beside him and snaked her arm around him, otherwise they'd both tumble off this small island of dirt. She gripped his thigh and together they pulled until his leg came free with a squelch.

They fell back on the ground. He wrapped his arms around her to keep her from sliding into the mud.

"Okay?" he asked.

Apart from being plastered against his hard body, she was fine. She nodded.

He looked over her shoulder. "Kantos is almost to the other side."

She let him help her up. "We need to keep moving—"

A gurgling sound rumbled behind them, and they both froze.

Together, they swiveled their heads.

A large, mud-covered creature rose out of the swamp.

Airen's pulse spiked. It was *huge*.

The creature had a humanoid body with a stocky middle, and short arms and legs. Mud dripped off its face and gaping mouth. It had two glowing red eyes.

"Oh, great," Donovan muttered.

The swamp creature let out a monstrous roar.

"SUGGESTIONS?" Donovan asked.

Airen glanced at him, her eyebrows rising. He saw surprise in her black-green eyes.

"I screwed up before by not listening to you," he said. "But I told you I'm a fast learner. How do we fight this?"

"I don't know exactly what this is, but the odds are good that it won't leave the swamp."

"So, we need to slow it down..."

"And get out of here."

"Okay, but first—" He grabbed her, yanked her close, and pressed a quick, hard kiss to her lips. "For luck."

She licked her lips and he tried to focus. Just that small taste of her was enough to scramble his brain. At that moment, his thumping pulse had little to do with the swamp creature.

Swamp creature. Imminent danger. *Right.*

He pulled out his laser pistol and fired. The mud creature jerked. Airen lifted her arm and morphed a weapon.

A green ball of energy hit the mud creature and it roared again, shaking its head. Mud splatter flew everywhere.

"Run!" Donovan yelled.

Airen took off, leaping from rock to small island to rock, elegant and graceful.

He followed, making sure he didn't slip off anything again. Suddenly, a large rock flew past them to land in the mud, splattering them both with mud.

*Dammit to hell.* He spun and fired his laser pistol.

The creature waved its arms around, enraged.

"Donovan, come *on*."

He turned and ran again. Ahead of him, Airen was almost at the edge of the swamp.

There was a whoosh of sound in the sky. He looked up and saw a Kantos swarm ship—a small, brown ship that reminded Donovan of a flea—fly overhead. It rose high, heading for space.

*Fuck.* The Kantos soldier had gotten away.

The swamp creature let out another roar.

Right behind him.

Donovan picked up speed. He was almost at Airen, and she raised her arm firing her blaster again.

He reached her, just as the mud creature flung itself at them.

Donovan tackled Airen off the rock she stood on. They flew through the air, then hit solid dirt at the edge of the swamp.

The swamp creature crashed into the mud nearby, spraying them both with a wave of smelly, brown goop.

It glared at them for a moment, then sank back into the muck.

Donovan wiped the mud off his face and looked at Airen.

She was coated with mud, as well.

The sound of people running through the forest made them both look up. Malax, Sabin, and several warriors appeared.

"We're fine." Airen shook her arm and mud splattered the grass.

Malax's lips twitched. "I hear mud has several beneficial qualities for your skin."

Donovan grunted and Airen frowned.

"Great time for you to find a sense of humor, War Commander," Donovan said.

Malax smiled. "I believe my mate is having an influence on me."

Airen rose. "We encountered a Kantos soldier. He got away."

The war commander's smile dissolved. "We saw the ship. I gave instructions for the *Rengard* to stop it."

Donovan knew it would be easy for one small swarm ship to evade the much larger warship.

"He might have stolen data," she said.

"The scientists told me that their system appears intact," Sabin said.

Airen blew out a breath, her shoulders dropping. "Okay. Good."

"Let's get back to the *Rengard,* so you two can clean up," Malax said.

When Donovan had wiped the worst of the mud off, he boarded the shuttle. He noted that Airen made sure she was nowhere near him. Two warriors were easily subduing a cursing, struggling pirate at the back of the shuttle. It was the man Donovan had shot out of a tree.

When the pirate saw him, the man sneered. Donovan ignored him.

On the ride back to the *Rengard,* the rest of the warriors gave Donovan a wide berth. Mostly because he smelled like crap. Donovan stared at the back of Airen's head and stewed. He was mad at himself. He'd screwed up with Airen, he'd apologized, but she still wasn't having it.

He scraped a hand through his hair. Damn, the mud was drying and his hair was crunchy.

Finally, they docked in the *Rengard's* shuttle bay. Airen was barking orders for them to secure the prisoner in the brig. She didn't glance Donovan's way once and his temper fraying, he decided to give her some space to cool down. He headed to his quarters and aimed straight for the shower. As the water pounded over him, he let his mind go blank. It took a long time for the water to run clear.

As he dried off, he looked at himself in the small washroom mirror. Okay, so he'd messed up. He'd said he was sorry. Now, all he could do was earn her trust back.

He pulled on a clean Space Corps uniform. Second Commander Airen Kann-Felis hadn't seen stubborn yet. He hesitated. He was getting in deep with this alien woman. He kept his relationships with women easy and friendly.

But what he felt for Airen went way beyond friendly. And the desire he had for her was potent, a little wild.

For a second, he was a boy again, lying in his bed and listening to his mother cry herself to sleep. She'd never dated, never re-married. She'd never stopped loving the asshole who'd abandoned her.

No, he wasn't obsessed with Airen. This attraction would burn out or fade eventually. Shoving the worry aside, he strode out of his cabin. When he entered the bridge, his gaze went straight to Airen.

No one would ever guess she'd been covered in mud

and fighting off a swamp creature less than an hour ago. She was clean, her black uniform spotless, her brown hair braided.

She turned her head and glanced at him like he was a piece of furniture, then looked back at the viewscreen.

*Stay calm.* Donovan moved toward her.

Malax strode out of his office. "We have another Eon ship on the way. They'll provide additional protection to the outpost and help them rebuild."

"Eon engineering ship, the *Structura*, inbound," a warrior called out.

A ship dropped out of starspeed and Donovan studied it. It wasn't a warship, so it was smaller than the *Rengard*, but like all Eon ships, it had a sleek, impressive design. It had several cranes built into the back of it, no doubt for in-space salvage and repairs.

He glanced at Airen and saw her jaw tighten.

The viewscreen blinked on to show an older warrior flanked by two male warriors.

Eon Warriors all looked very similar—muscular bodies and rugged facial features, and they wore their brown hair long. There were no blondes or black-haired Eon, just various shades of brown. And definitely none had skin as dark as Donovan.

"First Commander Lann-Ath, good to see you," Malax said. "The Thessa outpost will be grateful for the assistance of your team."

The first commander inclined his head. "Good to see you, War Commander Dann-Jad. You remember my second, Gavyn Narann-Felis, and my security commander, Ander Dann-Eon."

Malax nodded. "Welcome."

The security commander had a slightly prettier face, less rugged than most warriors. He turned his gaze to Airen.

"Airen, it is wonderful to see you again." The man's voice was a smooth drawl.

Donovan frowned at the man's over-friendly tone, a shiver skating down his spine.

"It's been a long time, Security Commander Dann-Eon." Her voice was devoid of any emotion.

*Fuck.* Realization dawned. *This* was the asshole. And he'd called her by her first name, not her title.

Donovan moved up behind her. There wasn't much he could do but offer his silent support. Hell, since she was angry with him, he doubted she'd welcome his support anyway. Without anyone seeing, he brushed his fingers against her back.

She didn't pull away.

"My Second Commander, Airen Kann-Felis, and our Security Commander, Sabin Solann-Ath," Malax said. "And our Terran ally, Sub-Captain Donovan Lennox."

Dann-Eon managed to drag his gaze off Airen. "Terran? Interesting." His tone said otherwise.

As he eyed Donovan, standing right behind her, the man's mouth tightened.

"I'm sending my engineering team to the surface," the first commander said. "While they make their initial assessment, let's meet, Malax. Let our command team mingle and discuss what needs to be done for the outpost before the *Rengard* heads off again."

"Excellent," Malax said. "You're all invited aboard the *Rengard*."

"I hope we get to meet your new mate."

Malax smiled. "Of course."

"I'll be careful not to let her hijack my ship," First Commander Lann-Ath said with a smile.

Malax shot the man a rueful smile. "That's an excellent idea. My mate is a woman of many talents."

# CHAPTER SIX

---

Warriors filled the large conference room on the *Rengard*.

It wasn't a party. They were talking about the reconstruction work at the outpost, and about the Kantos.

Regardless, Airen just wanted it over with so she could get back to work. They had the pirate prisoner in the brig, and she wanted to question him.

There was more to this attack, she was sure of it.

She glanced over and saw Malax introducing Wren around. The Terran was smiling and, in usual Wren fashion, charming First Commander Lann-Ath without even trying to.

"Airen."

Ander's voice behind her. It made her want to wrinkle her nose.

She turned. "Ander."

He looked good—smooth and handsome. She'd found that attractive when she'd first met him, but now his face seemed a little...soft.

"It's wonderful to see you," he said.

She didn't respond. She certainly didn't feel the same way.

He glanced around, admiring some of the ornamental weapons on the wall. "You must enjoy your work here on the *Rengard*. It's a magnificent ship."

She saw it now. His envy. It was her promotion to second commander of the *Rengard* that was the death of their relationship. He'd called her too driven, too unbending, too independent.

For a second, she had a flash of Donovan's face and his blatant admiration of her fighting skills.

Ander had been jealous. She realized that now. Ander had always been all about Ander.

She looked past him, barely listening as he droned on. She spotted Donovan among the crowd, his dark skin so smooth. He looked good in his dark-blue Space Corps uniform.

He looked up and their gazes met. Then he glared at Ander.

She'd known Terrans worked differently to the Eon. They could be orderly, they had rules, but they often went off plan, and were creative and spontaneous.

She'd also met Donovan's captain, Allie Borden. The woman was bold and confident, and now mated to Second Commander Brack Thann-Felis of the *Desteron*. Airen could see Allie allowing Donovan more leeway to bend the rules on a mission.

Airen sighed. She hadn't really accepted his apology, or let him explain. Still, it was best they kept things professional between them.

"Airen?"

*Cren*, she'd completely forgotten about Ander. "Sorry. I've got lots on my mind."

"Of course." He leaned closer, his voice dropping to an intimate drawl. "I've missed you."

*Seriously?* She looked into his black eyes streaked with gold. "Really?"

"Yes. We were good together."

She blinked. He had a creative memory. *Cren*, she was so not interested in this. "I heard that you were engaged to be married."

He straightened, his lips tipping up. "Are you keeping tabs on me?"

"No. Someone mentioned it in passing."

"It's an advantageous marriage. She's a teacher." He gave a small laugh. "Well, almost a teacher. She finishes at the academy at the end of the year."

So, the poor woman was young. Airen found she felt...nothing.

She hadn't loved Ander deeply or passionately. She'd just wanted a connection. And then she'd let him push the right buttons to make her doubt her strength.

"Well, I wish you both well."

Ander frowned. "Marriage doesn't mean I'm not free to be with you when it suits us. My soon-to-be wife and I have an understanding."

By the warriors, what had Airen ever seen in this man? "Actually, Ander, it does. Marriage is a commitment."

"But you'll never mate, never marry—"

She cocked her head. "Why do you say that?"

He looked at her askance. "You've never wanted that. You're so driven, dedicated to your career."

"So? If I find the right man, one who supports me in all that I am and want to do, and can handle my strength..." She shrugged. "That was just never you."

Now his eyes narrowed. "Good luck finding a man like that. No man, especially a warrior, likes to be emasculated, Airen."

She felt a warm, solid presence at her back. She smelled Donovan, but she already knew it was him. It was like she could sense him.

"Ander, you've met Donovan."

The security commander's mouth firmed. "A pleasure. I hope you're not too overwhelmed here aboard the *Rengard*."

"Seriously?" Donovan looked down at Airen. "You were with this guy?"

She shrugged one shoulder. "I'm wondering why, myself."

Donovan smiled and it was dazzling. Her gaze dropped to his mouth.

"You busting to question that pirate?" he asked.

She nodded. "Yes."

"Can we blow this gathering now?"

"I think so."

Ander cleared his throat. "Excuse me, we were talking."

"You're done." Donovan rested his hand on Airen's shoulder.

He didn't push in front of her, or talk over her, or try

to intimidate Ander. Just a confident man, sure of himself, offering her quiet support.

"I wish you the best of luck with your marriage, Ander."

"Airen, a Terran? Really, you'd lower yourself to this?"

The anger that cut through her was sharp.

Donovan arched a brow. "I feel so insulted." His tone was deadpan.

She found herself fighting off a smile.

"You're *nothing*," Ander continued. "You're from a low-tech, backwater planet—"

Donovan leaned down to Airen. "Maybe we should introduce him to Eve and Lara?"

Oh, the deadly Traynor sisters would just love Ander. "Maybe for the sake of our alliance, we shouldn't. Ander, I realize you need to belittle everyone to make yourself feel better, but we have an alliance with the Terrans, and you will show Donovan respect."

Ander scoffed.

She lowered her voice. "Donovan is ten times the man you are."

The warrior stiffened and made a spluttering sound.

Malax stepped into their group. "What are we discussing here?"

Ander stiffened and clamped his mouth shut.

"Nothing important," Airen said. "Donovan and I are heading down to interrogate the pirate prisoner."

Malax nodded. "Keep me updated."

She looked at Donovan, who was still grinning. "Ready?"

"Oh yeah, lead the way, Second Commander."

---

DONOVAN TRIED to gauge how Airen was feeling, but her face looked calm and composed.

They rounded a corner in the corridor. "Are you okay?"

"You know what?" she said. "I'm better than okay. Ander is, to borrow an Earth word, an asshole."

Donovan snorted. "You've got that right." As they neared the brig, he grabbed her arm. "I made a mistake not listening to you on the outpost mission, but I'm not like that jackass—"

Airen pressed a finger to his lips. "I know."

A sense of relief flooded him. "I'm going to earn your trust back."

"Everything's fine, Donovan. We have a good working relationship."

He moved his lips against her finger and she sucked in a breath.

"Maybe a little more than a working relationship?" he said.

"No."

"God, I really want to kiss you, Airen."

"That's not appropriate—"

"So be inappropriate, just for a second."

"I was once. With Ander."

Donovan scowled. "Don't compare me to that—"

Airen surprised him by yanking him close and kissing him.

*Oh, yeah.* The taste of her was exquisite. He opened his mouth, and touched his tongue to hers.

She slid her arms around his shoulders and moaned.

But Donovan was conscious that they were right near the brig, and anyone could see them. She'd hate that.

He lifted her up and stalked into a shadowed side corridor, pressing her against the wall. She moaned into his mouth again, and they kissed like they needed each other to survive.

Finally, she lifted her head. She was panting, and several strands of her hair had escaped her braid.

"What was that?" she murmured.

"No idea." It was hot and desperate, and better than any kiss he'd ever had before.

She wiggled and he set her on the floor. She straightened her uniform. "I've no idea where we were going. My brain's short-circuited."

Donovan grinned. "I don't believe that for a second."

"Okay, I remember the pirate, but my brain really is scrambled."

"Mine too."

"We aren't doing it again," she said in a stern voice.

"Okay," he agreed readily.

She squinted suspiciously at him. "You agreed very quickly."

"Well, you had already told me before that we wouldn't do it again, but you've kissed the hell out of me a couple of times now." He smiled. "And I'm going to be right at your side, reminding you of the goodness you're missing out on. I think I might even spoil you a little bit, might be fun."

She scowled. "Is this a seduction tactic of yours? Do you do this with all women?"

"Hell, no. I don't usually need to put much effort into it at all."

Her eyes narrowed and he decided to not dwell on that point.

He touched her hair. "I think you're worth it, Second Commander."

"How would you know how to spoil a woman, then?"

"I have three sisters."

She shook her head. "No spoiling, no kissing. We have work to do."

"I know."

"And I don't have time for a dalliance. Ander was right, I have a demanding job to do, and I—"

"I won't be around forever, Airen. I've no desire to have what Malax and Wren have." Although, saying that strangely made his throat tighten.

She eyed him steadily. "Really?"

"Really. Love isn't real, it doesn't last, and it hurts people."

"Malax and Wren love each other and are very happy. Her sisters, Allie—"

"All exceptions that prove the rule, plus there's the whole mating thing that makes their connections different. I watched my father leave, and it tore my mom to shreds. She cried every night for years. Love ruined her."

Airen's brows drew together. "Donovan—"

"He left and she never stopped loving him. It made her desperately unhappy. No, not interested in that. Two of my sisters have been married, and divorced. One of the assholes beat my sister."

"You stopped him," Airen said quietly.

"I broke his jaw and took her home. Love is a lie we use to make ourselves feel good—but it's temporary." He reached up and brushed his thumb across her tempting lips. "Good, honest desire and respect. I'll take that any day."

She eyed him a little longer. "We need to interrogate the pirate."

Even though it was hard, Donovan stepped back. "Let's do it."

When they entered the brig, the warriors in charge nodded at Airen.

The pirate was in a cell, sitting on a bare bunk behind a shimmering containment field. Airen stepped through it, and then Donovan followed. A slight tingle ran over his skin.

The pirate looked at them sulkily. "Space-cursed Eon, always so high and mighty."

He had a scarred face, ragged clothes, and cloudy, green eyes.

"We are," Airen said. "Especially when you attack our outposts, and kill and injure our people."

The pirate sniffed. "Just wanted to get your attention."

"Well, you've got it. And I guarantee you won't like the results."

"Why did you attack?" Donovan asked.

"The Kantos paid us. They're ugly suckers, but their credits are good."

"What was the objective?" Airen demanded. "To steal something? Our data?"

"Nope." The pirate slouched back, like he didn't have a care in the universe.

Annoyed, Donovan kicked the man's boots. "Answer her. Why the fuck did you attack?"

"The Kantos wanted us to."

"Why?" Airen snapped.

Cloudy eyes glanced at Donovan, then back to Airen. "So you'd come."

Donovan frowned, saw Airen frowning as well.

"So the *Rengard* would come?" she asked.

"Nope. You. Second Commander Airen Kann-Felis."

Donovan's gut clenched. *What the fuck?*

# CHAPTER SEVEN

"Explain," Airen demanded.

She didn't take her eyes off the pirate. *They'd come here looking for her?* It made no sense.

"I don't know any more than that." The pirate grinned, showing dirty, decaying teeth. "Just get a female warrior to Thessa. We made a big mess, that's how we like it."

"Get her there and then what?" Donovan's voice was low, scary.

That dangerous edge made the pirate's smile dissolve. "Tell him to back off."

"Do I make you nervous?" Donovan's silky drawl put goose bumps on Airen's skin.

"Donovan," she warned.

"Why do the Kantos want her?" Donovan continued. "I'm particularly fond of her, and I want to know."

"They want her. That's all I know. Our old leader, Arnaf, he would know more."

"Arnaf?" Airen asked.

"He was in charge of our clan when we got the job, but he didn't really want to come after the Eon. Credits were too good, though. We had a little mutiny and a leadership change. We dumped Arnaf on the way here, and Cyris took over. He's dead now, down on the planet."

Donovan looked at Airen.

"Where did you dump this Arnaf?" she asked.

"Old, abandoned mining colony." The pirate got a cagey look on his face. "You let me go, I'll tell you the coordinates."

Donovan leaned in. "Just tell us, so I don't have to beat the shit out of you." His smile turned scary. "Actually, I wouldn't mind beating the shit out of you."

"Suck space cock, you—"

Donovan gripped the pirate's neck and slammed his face into the table. The pirate howled.

"Let's try this again," Airen said calmly.

"Fine, fine." The pirate touched the small trickle of blood coming from his nose, then glared at Donovan. "Tell him to back up."

Donovan just crossed his arms over his chest.

"Talk," Airen said.

"Fine, I'll tell you the coordinates. You have to go in quietly, or he'll run."

After the pirate shared the coordinates, things moved fast. Airen went to brief Malax, and the war commander nodded.

"We have repairs well underway, so we can spare you. It is imperative we find out what the Kantos are planning."

"I'll take a shuttle. It's best I go alone so I don't spook—"

"No. It's too dangerous. The Kantos appear to want you, Airen."

She straightened. "I can handle the Kantos, Malax."

"I know, but you take Donovan. Two Eon might appear a threat. A Terran, maybe not so much."

Internally, she cursed. It wasn't that she didn't trust Donovan's skills. She just preferred that he stayed safe on the *Rengard*.

"You two work well together," Malax said.

"He is extremely competent."

"Terrans are full of surprises." A small smile flirted on Malax's lips. "Report in, and good hunting."

Airen found Donovan waiting for her in the corridor.

"Malax is sending you and me to the coordinates," she told him.

He grinned. "So, just the two of us?"

She shot him a look as they headed down the corridor. "We'll be working."

It didn't take long before they were prepped and in the shuttle.

Airen did the pre-flight checks, with Donovan watching on with interest. The man seemed to absorb everything.

"Didn't know you were a pilot too," he said.

"We all take basic piloting courses at the academy. I took a few advanced ones. I like flying." As a young girl, she'd desperately wanted the freedom to soar.

"Me too. Always dreamed of flying through space as a kid."

Their gazes met, a shared moment.

Then she turned her attention to the controls. Soon, they were flying out of the shuttle bay doors. As they moved out into space, she tapped in the coordinates for the mining colony, and the ship turned sharply. Then they sped away from the *Rengard*.

"It's not too far. A ship hour to reach the coordinates at star speed."

"Where is this mining colony?" he asked. "A planet? A moon?"

"Star charts show a small asteroid field. Asteroid mining is risky, but pretty common out here. The asteroids are packed full of valuable ores."

"Perfect spot to dump someone when you carry out a mutiny." Donovan paused. "I don't like this, Airen. The Kantos are after you."

She didn't like it either. "I don't know why, but I plan to find out."

"Looks like oh-so-smooth Ander won't be able to corner you and drip his slime around."

Donovan's sharp words made her bite back a smile. "I'm not disappointed. He's getting married and thought I'd be interested in having an affair." She shook her head.

Donovan's face went tight. "So not just an idiot, but a cheater as well."

"I'm sure he sees his marriage as a merger of convenience. No doubt her family has influence." Which he'd always taken great pains to remind her she didn't have.

Reaching out, Donovan touched her hand. "The guy is so far beneath you, Airen."

Warmth flooded her. "Thanks." She fiddled with the controls. "So, you don't believe in love?"

He leaned back in his chair. "No. Not romantic love. Love is destructive. It makes people lose their sense of reason, and it hurts." His gaze turned inward, no doubt thinking of his mother and sisters.

"I believe in love," Airen said quietly. "I just don't think I'd ever trust anyone with my desires and feelings enough to fall in love." She shot him a tight smile. "Everyone who should have loved me, left me."

Something moved across his face. "Airen—"

The console chimed. "We're in range."

It wasn't long before the asteroid field came into view.

"Fuck," Donovan muttered. "How will we find where they dumped him?"

"There's likely some processing facilities here somewhere. We'll check the larger asteroids." She tapped the controls. "Initiating scans now. *There*. There's a beacon signal still running. It would have led the ore transports in."

They moved into the field. The asteroids weren't too dense, but smaller debris pinged off the shuttle's shields. A huge asteroid moved past them like a silent behemoth.

Then Airen saw another large hunk of rock ahead. "Look."

There were some metallic structures on the surface, but not many. The risk of collision with other asteroids was too high. There was a large, rectangular opening that led inside the asteroid's core.

"Most of the mining facilities are inside the asteroid," she said.

Donovan frowned. "That's expensive construction. I wonder why they abandoned it?"

"Maybe they ran out of ore?"

He swiped the control panel in front of him. "Scans show large concentrations of several different ores."

"A mystery." She focused on flying them inside.

They passed through the entrance into pitch blackness. The shuttle's lights speared into the darkness, illuminating rock walls braced with metal supports.

It wasn't much farther and the tunnel opened up into a large hanger area. They passed through the shimmer of a containment field.

"Containment's still operational," Donovan said.

"Most containment systems like this run on backup systems. They don't need to be maintained. They'll run until their fuel cores deplete."

Two ships in decent condition were docked. There was a third one that had been stripped for parts, possibly by the pirates.

She set the shuttle down.

Donovan tapped the console. "Conditions are just barely in the breathable range. Oxygen's on the low side."

"Helmets on." She rose from her chair. "Let's find our exiled pirate."

They exited the shuttle and, as they moved onto a walkway, lights clicked on, illuminating the path to a building constructed within the rock walls. It was all metal and glass.

"Spooky as hell," Donovan muttered.

There was no sound and nothing moved.

They stepped inside the building, but there were no lights. As Donovan flicked on a flashlight, Airen morphed a light on the shoulder of her armor.

"Fuck," he muttered.

She followed his gaze and saw what was illuminated by his flashlight. A dead, decayed body sat slumped against the wall. The dead man's chest had been ripped open.

Bloody handprints covered the wall.

Airen scanned the space. There were more dead bodies in the shadows. Lots of them.

"Well, it appears the miners didn't abandon this place," she said. "They never got the chance to leave."

---

THERE WAS no sign of recent occupation. Donovan swung his flashlight around.

Damn, this place creeped him out.

In the lobby area, furniture was tipped over and items were scattered around. There were more dead bodies.

He crouched by one, studying it. The man had been big, burly. It hadn't stopped his death.

"Looks like his heart was ripped out."

Airen's face remained impassive, but he sensed her disquiet. "If the pirate's living here, he'd need quarters, food, water."

"Let's find the barracks," Donovan said.

They moved out of the lobby area and through some large, double doors into what was a processing area. Huge equipment filled the space—conveyors, cranes attached to the rocky ceiling overhead, huge vats that no doubt had once held processing chemicals.

Airen walked along one of the conveyors and pulled out a handheld scanner. "It looks like they were mining several different ores." She frowned. "There's one here that I don't have on record."

"They found something new?"

"Apparently. There are only residual quantities."

A clanking noise sounded nearby and they both swiveled. Donovan lifted his laser pistol.

There was silence.

"You ever seen a horror movie, Airen?" he murmured.

"No." She moved deeper into the shadows.

He followed her. "Unsuspecting people walk into a dark space, then get attacked and murdered."

Her sword formed. "I prefer to do the attacking."

No fear. Damn, she was something.

They circled around a conveyor, and he spotted a tool resting on the ground. No sign of anybody near it.

They kept moving. Damn, he couldn't wait to get out of here.

A low moan echoed through the area.

"My helian is detecting a life sign," Airen said.

He tightened his grip on his pistol. *Come out, come out, wherever you are.*

A shape rushed out of the shadows from between two vats.

"What the fuck?" Donovan snapped.

It was humanoid, with extra-long arms almost dragging on the ground and a misshapen skull. Its skin was a sickly, mottled gray and it had ragged, ripped clothing hanging off its body. A huge hump sat on one shoulder, giving it a lopsided appearance.

The creature's face was covered in tumor-like growths. It opened its mouth—showing off what looked like shark's teeth.

It let out a howling moan, and Donovan fired. He kept firing. The creature's body jerked and shuddered under the impact of the laser, but it kept coming.

Airen ran, jumped, and swung her sword.

The creature dodged, then swung out a long arm at her.

Its fist hit her and she flew sideways, crashing into a vat with a *clang*.

Donovan shoved his pistol away and yanked out his knife. "Hey!"

The thing swiveled, gaze locking on him. It came at him fast. It swiped out and Donovan ducked one of those huge fists, then slammed his elbow into the creature's head. His knife flashed as he attacked.

With a low moan, it pulled back, stumbling a little.

"Airen?" Donovan didn't take his gaze off the creature.

"I'm okay."

He'd cut the thing. The ugly ooze of red-green blood dripped down its torso.

"What is it?" Donovan said.

"I don't know, but I'm detecting some residual radiation from it."

*Radiation?* But he didn't have time to think, because it launched itself at them again.

"With me," Donovan yelled. "Let's work it together."

Airen appeared beside him. She slashed at the creature, and when she drew back, Donovan launched in. The thing moaned, trying to swing at them. They drove it back across the mining processing area.

Ahead, Donovan spotted a large vat, partly tilted over. Its foundations were loose.

"Airen, look."

She swung her sword and glanced up. "I see it. You keep this thing busy and get it into position."

She darted away and Donovan circled the creature. It snapped its teeth at him.

"Yeah, yeah, you want to tear me open and eat my heart. Not today, buddy."

Walking backward, he moved the creature closer to the vat. With a moan, it rushed him and Donovan lifted a boot and kicked it, hard. It staggered, but righted itself. The creature came at him again, like a racecar in the closing stretch.

*Fuck.*

Donovan kicked it again, but it was ready for him this time. It grabbed his boot and yanked.

*Dammit.* Donovan was pulled off his feet. The creature swung him and let go. Donovan hit the floor and slid across the concrete, right in line with the vat.

He moved to jump up, but the creature landed on top of him.

*Shit.* It was heavy as hell, driving the air out of him. Its teeth snapped at Donovan's helmet. He shoved it, managing to lift his knife. He stabbed into the creature's gut.

With a moaning growl, it headbutted him. A small crack appeared in his helmet.

Not good.

"Donovan!" Airen yelled.

He looked up, shoving at the creature's chest. Over its shoulder, he saw the vat teetering, starting to fall.

It would land right on them.

Adrenaline spiked through him. He heaved with everything he had and shoved the creature off him.

Then he pushed himself up, trying to get out of the way of the falling vat.

"Donovan!"

Airen was running at him.

"Stay back," he warned.

He was just about clear, but something grabbed his ankle. The creature yanked him down with a growl.

Donovan slammed facefirst onto the ground. He kicked at the creature, trying to get free.

The huge metal vat descended faster.

Then firm fingers closed on Donovan's hand. He looked up to see Airen right in front of him. She pulled, sliding him across the floor. The creature lost its grip on his ankle.

Freed, Donovan shoved up and rolled, knocking into Airen. They landed on the ground, him on top of her.

Only a meter away from them, the vat crashed down —right on top of the creature.

# CHAPTER EIGHT

Airen's heart raced. Donovan had been *so* close to being crushed by the vat. His helmet clicked against hers.

"I really want to kiss you right now," he said.

Her heart gave another hard squeeze. "I really want you to kiss me, too."

He groaned.

"You have a crack in your helmet."

"It's holding. Just no more wrestling with strange monsters that want to eat me." He pushed himself up and took her hand, pulling her to her feet.

"So, what the hell was that thing?" He glanced back at the overturned vat.

"I'm not sure. I'm just hoping there aren't any more of them. Let's keep searching for our pirate."

"Airen, he might be dead."

"Well, we keep looking until we know for sure."

"And keep an eye out for other monsters lurking around."

She scanned their surroundings. "I'm not detecting anything." Her scanner beeped and she frowned. "There are low levels of radiation."

"Dangerous?"

"No."

They moved along the conveyor. Ore was still stacked on the belt, glimmering under their lights.

"This is the unidentified ore. It's showing higher levels of radiation, the same as the creature." Horror moved through her. "Donovan, I think they had some sort of accident with this ore."

"And some of them were exposed to it, irradiated?"

She nodded.

"Hell." He pressed his hands to his hips, looking around with a grim face.

"It appears to be safe now, but let's not disturb the ore."

"There had to be hundreds of miners working here." He met her gaze. "That's a lot of monsters."

They continued on, moving through a doorway.

"Living quarters," she said.

They moved inside, heading toward a set of stairs that led up to an open, second level. She swung her light through the dark space and the beam bounced off many doors. The central area must have been an eating and relaxing space. It was a mess—with furniture overturned, and litter on the ground.

A sound echoed above them and they both tensed.

She spotted a flash of movement as someone darted up the stairs.

Donovan broke into a sprint.

*Cren.* She ran after him.

They pounded up the stairs and she wondered if it was another monster.

They reached the top and Donovan dived, tackling a lean figure.

"Let me go!"

Donovan pinned the man and Airen stood over him, shining the light down.

"Eon," the man spat.

Definitely their pirate. He was older, with scraggly, gray hair and a lined face. It was clear he'd lived a hard, rough life. He wasn't wearing a helmet and appeared to be working harder to breathe.

"We aren't here to hurt you, Arnaf," she said.

"Well, you two made enough noise that the space-cursed monsters will be here to eat us all any minute now." He drew in some harsh breaths. "Already hard enough for me to breath in here, especially if I have to run."

"How many of them?" Donovan asked.

"I don't know," the pirate grumbled. "Enough. Ten, maybe."

"You've been hiding from them?" she asked.

"Ever since my cowardly, backstabbing men dumped me here. When I get my hands on Cyris—"

"He's dead." Donovan levered himself off the pirate.

The old man paused. "No great loss."

"They're all dead. Bar one in the brig aboard an Eon warship. He told us where to find you."

"Idiots took the Kantos job." The pirate cursed, and for a second, looked sad. His face firmed and he glanced at Airen. "I told them attacking an Eon outpost was a stupid idea."

"Well, wherever they are now, I'm sure they're regretting the decision," she said.

"You're the female warrior the bugs wanted. Kann-Felis."

"That's why we are here. We need to know what you know. Why do they want me?"

"You gonna get me off this rock?"

Donovan crossed his arms. "If the info is good."

"They want your helian." The pirate's gaze dropped to her wristband.

"You can't remove a bonded helian without killing both the host and the helian," she said.

The pirate sucked on one of his teeth. "Bugs think they can. At least, with a female Eon."

Airen felt a wave of something horrible wash over her. "What?"

The pirate shrugged. "Something about being female, your biology, makes 'em think they can do it."

Donovan cursed.

Breathing deeply, she pushed her concern and anger down. "We need to go." She needed to warn the other female Eon warriors, just in case the Kantos came after them. This *couldn't* be true. She didn't want it to be true.

"Come on." Donovan pushed the pirate ahead of them. They headed down the stairs.

They moved out into the dark processing area, and guttural moans echoed through the space. A lot of moans.

Airen's blood fired.

"Fuck," Donovan bit out. "We have a lot of company incoming."

"Run," Airen said.

They sprinted across the space. Ahead, a crowd of monsters—misshapen beings, all different shapes and sizes—appeared out of the gloom, stumbling toward them.

Donovan whipped his laser pistol up and fired.

Airen spotted the door ahead, but it was still too far away. They wouldn't make it before the monsters cut them off.

The pirate let out a wild yell and yanked a clunky, homemade explosive off his belt. "Go!"

"I promised to get you out of here," Airen said.

"I'm old, and I got nowhere to go." He lifted the explosive. "My clan's all dead. I might as well go out with a bang and take as many of these monsters with me as I can."

The pirate spun, and ran toward the irradiated creatures.

"Come on." Donovan grabbed her hand.

Together, they sprinted into the lobby area.

*Boom.*

She heard the explosion behind them, felt the subsequent shockwave.

She sucked in a breath. *Thank you, Arnaf.*

They ran out of the building and sprinted down the walkway to the ship. They dived inside the shuttle, and Donovan closed the door behind them.

"Get us out of here, Second Commander."

Through the viewscreen, she saw the monsters

coming. She fired up the engines. "My pleasure."

---

DONOVAN GLANCED at Airen in the pilot seat. She was silent, tension humming around her.

"We're locked on course to the *Rengard* and at star speed." Her tone was wooden.

"You okay?"

She blew out a breath. "That pirate sacrificed himself for us."

"Well, I got the impression he usually did things for his own good. He knew he had nowhere to go, and that his pirate clan was all gone."

She was silent for a moment. "The Kantos might have a way to extract my helian." She shuddered.

Donovan reached over and grabbed her hand. He rubbed his thumb over her wrist, brushing her helian band. "That's not going to happen."

"We need to warn all the female warriors."

"Once we're back, we will."

"I keep thinking of those poor miners."

"Yeah." He squeezed her hand. "Poor bastards."

"I'll have Malax inform the appropriate authorities." She stood and started pacing the small craft. "Right now, I want to destroy the Kantos. They want to extract my helian, destroy the Eon, annihilate Earth—"

Her cheeks were flushed, and Donovan decided he much preferred her angry to sad and upset. Apparently, Airen had a hidden temper.

"That's my warrior," he said.

She turned to look at him. "You like it when I'm ruthless and tough."

He leaned back in his seat. "It's sexy as hell, Airen."

"Ander felt threatened."

Donovan smiled, not wanting to think about that asshole. "Do I look threatened?"

She stepped closer. "No."

There was a flare of green threads in her eyes, glowing turquoise.

Fire and passion lived within Airen Kann-Felis. She hid it well under her skill and discipline, but it was there.

"Back on the asteroid, when the vat fell, I thought I was about to lose you," she said.

His blood heated. "I'm fine."

She stalked closer. "I really want to kiss you right now."

His cock went hard in an instant. "That's my line."

Then the gorgeous Eon warrior shocked him by straddling him, right there in the cockpit seat.

He put his hands on her hips. "Airen—"

"I want to stop thinking, Donovan. I want to bend those rules you often ignore."

She sank onto him. At the contact of their bodies, desire was a rushing flood inside him. He slid one hand into her hair. "What else do you want? Tell me, and I'll give it to you."

"Maybe I want you to take it," she whispered.

With a growl, he pulled her head down. He opened her lips and plunged his tongue inside her sweet mouth. She moaned, shimmying against him.

The world—or rather, the universe—ceased to exist. There was just Airen—sweet, hot, sexy Airen.

The kiss was wild and held an edge. He bit her lip and she moaned, grinding her slim, toned body on his cock.

*Shit.* He struggled not to come there and then.

"Open it," he growled.

"What?" she breathed.

"My suit."

She licked her lips and touched the fastening at the neck of his spacesuit. It parted, baring his chest and she made a hungry sound.

"Touch me," he ordered.

She didn't hesitate. She splayed her hands against his pecs, her fingers digging into his dark skin. "I love your body. Your muscles, your skin."

He groaned. He knew that Airen spent all day giving orders, but right now, in his arms, she didn't hesitate to do as he asked. "Take your armor off."

She hesitated for a second, and he kissed her—hard, deep, drawing the taste of her inside him.

The black scales started to melt away, sliding down her torso. It uncovered a black tank underneath.

He reached up and tugged it down, until her breasts popped free. She arched into him, and he leaned forward and licked one pink nipple.

"*Donovan.*"

"So damn sexy, Airen."

Her lips parted, her eyes bright. "No one's ever said that before."

Dann-Eon was an idiot. "Then every man you know is a fool."

He pulled her closer and sucked her nipple into his mouth.

"Oh..." She moaned. She undulated against him again, grinding on his cock.

*Damn.* He fought to hold onto his slipping control. "You drive me wild."

"Same. Donovan, it's..."

He licked and sucked, her pretty nipples now hard points. "What? Tell me?"

She moaned his name. "I'm hot, out of control."

"You're gorgeous."

He slid his hand down and cupped her ass. She pushed against his palm.

"Feel how hard I am? That's all for you. All your fault."

He took her mouth again and she moved faster, breathing quickening.

"Donovan—"

"I want you to come, sexy girl. Keep rubbing against me, take what you need."

"I couldn't, not like this."

"Wanna bet?"

He cupped her ass and urged her on, grinding her down, hard. Her face flushed, her turquoise-and-black gaze on his face.

"Get there, Airen."

She was rocking hard against him now. His cock was like steel, but he wanted to see her pleasure.

Then she stiffened. "Donovan—"

He kissed her. As her orgasm hit her, he kept kissing her, feeling her pleasure, tasting it.

When her body stopped shuddering, she pressed her face to his neck. He stroked her back.

"That was...inappropriate," she said.

"Totally. Can we do it again?"

She lifted her head and smiled.

Damn, he could get used to that smile. He felt a skitter of warning through his head, but ignored it. He reached out and rubbed his thumb across her lips.

"Perhaps it was inappropriate," she said. "But not wrong."

"No, it felt pretty darn right."

Her hand slid down his body. "And now I want—"

Alarms started blaring and Airen jolted. "*Cren.*"

As she leaped up, her armor started reforming. Donovan frowned, refastening his suit. He swiped at the console.

Swirls of color appeared on the viewscreen. It was right in front of their ship. *What the hell was that?*

"What is it?" he barked.

She swiped the console and sucked in a sharp breath. "It's some sort of anomaly."

"Are we under attack? Is it the Kantos?"

Her gaze crashed into his. "It's a wormhole. We're being sucked into a wormhole."

# CHAPTER NINE

The ship shuddered and jerked, accelerating fast. Dizziness washed over Airen.

Colors streamed past the viewscreen like a waterfall.

"Controls aren't responding," Donovan yelled.

The wormhole spat them out and disappeared as quickly as it came. Their shuttle spun sideways, fully unchecked. Airen fought to gain some control.

She cursed. "We're losing an engine."

"Fuck."

Muffled explosions came from the back of the ship, and the shuttle shuddered again.

Airen felt her harness dig into her shoulders. She pressed her palm to the console. A line snaked out of her armor and, through her helian, she plugged straight into the ship's systems.

She straightened, the helian working through the data at lightning speed.

"I'm working to contain an engine fire."

Something else flared in her consciousness, her helian pulsing urgently. Airen gasped. *Oh, no.*

"What is it?" Donovan asked.

"We have company."

He tried his console again, then thumped his fist against it. "Work, damn you."

Airen ordered her helian to repair the console and it flared to life.

She glanced at it briefly, knowing that it would show a cloud of Kantos swarm ships arrowing toward them.

"Goddammit." Donovan tapped and swiped, his fingers moving fast. "I need weapons."

"I can—"

"You need to focus on flying the ship and keeping us operational." His smile was blinding white. "I'll shoot those insect fuckers down."

Airen found that she liked Donovan's fierceness. What you saw was what you got with Donovan Lennox.

She continued to work on repairs and keep the ship moving. The swarm ships dominated their viewscreen, closing in.

The Kantos' ships were all insect-like, with an organic look, and lots of protuberances.

Donovan fired and lasers arced through the sky. The swarm ships evaded—dipping and spinning like a cloud of insects.

Several of the ships exploded and her heart thumped against her chest. She pulled the shuttle up hard. Several swarm ships pulled in behind them, giving chase.

*Cren.* One of her engines was laboring, affecting their speed and maneuverability.

The shuttle jerked, throwing them forward against their harnesses. Her helian pulsed, and the console lit up with alarms.

"We've lost an engine," she cried.

Donovan leaned over his console, focused on fighting off the swarm ships. "There are too many of them." He smacked his palm against the console. "And the shuttle doesn't have enough firepower."

She gritted her teeth, fighting to keep the ship flying. Pain spiked down her spine. She knew she was overdoing it, but if she stopped, they were dead.

There was another volley from the swarm ships and she threw them into evasive maneuvers. In the distance, she saw a larger Kantos battlecruiser appear.

"They aren't shooting us down." Donovan met her gaze. "They're just disabling us."

A bad taste filled her mouth. "They want me alive."

"Well they can fuck off." He swiped his console again, his jaw tight.

"Donovan—"

"No. I will *not* let them take you, Airen. Over my dead body."

She jolted. The thought of Donovan dead...

*No.* Not happening.

"I've got a planet on scanners," he said.

"What? Where?" Ahead was just empty space.

He barked out the coordinates and her belly tightened. It wasn't far, but it wasn't very close, either.

In a damaged shuttle, they might make it, but with Kantos swarm ships chasing them, it was highly unlikely.

"Donovan—"

He reached out and grabbed her hand. "We can make it."

His golden gaze was unwavering, filling her with hope. She nodded.

She turned their ship. She pulled as much speed as she could from the faltering final engine. Pain flared through her body as she strained her connection to the ship, but she wasn't giving up.

Donovan kept firing, trying to keep the swarm ships back. Another volley of Kantos fire hit them, tossing them both in the seats. Smoke filled the cockpit.

Ahead, the planet came into view. It was a large, dark-blue orb.

"I've got no idea where we are," he said. "Star charts don't match anything close to where we were."

"The wormhole could have spat us out anywhere," she said.

"The Kantos generated it."

"Yes." A worry for another time. The Eon had experimented with wormhole technology, but they couldn't generate one large enough to swallow a starship. That the Kantos could was very upsetting.

"It's an aquatic planet," Donovan said. "Mostly water, but there are a few chains of rocky, mountainous islands."

Okay, that didn't sound too bad.

"There's some volcanic activity, and the ocean is teeming with life signs. Big ones."

She wrinkled her nose. Not great, but nothing too concerning.

"There are some very small settlements. One more

technologically advanced location. It's heavily fortified, has a spaceport, and it's pumping some sort of energy into the atmosphere."

Now, a shiver ran down Airen's spine. *No, it couldn't be.*

"Airen? I'm getting pretty good at reading your blank looks, and I know something's up."

"We can't go there."

"We have no choice. It's the only option—"

"I know what this planet is. We're well outside of Eon space."

"What is it?"

"Oblivion." She swallowed. "It's a prison planet."

A muscle ticked in his jaw. "Prison planet?"

"The most brutal one I know. Several systems dump their worst of the worst here. The oceans are filled with genetically-engineered creatures designed to keep the prisoners under control. When the prisoners aren't slaughtering each other."

Another laser volley hit, and they both jerked. There were more alarms and more clouds of smoke. Airen coughed.

"They have some sort of security net in place around the planet. It's a bad place, Donovan." She coughed again and another alarm started ringing like crazy. "We've lost our last engine!"

The ship spun, the dizzying roll throwing her back in her seat.

Oblivion rose up in front of them—dark and forbidding.

"It's Oblivion or the Kantos," Donovan said. "And I don't think we have a choice anymore."

They hit the planet's atmosphere, flames flaring up over the viewscreen. The ship shook so hard that Airen felt like her bones were breaking.

Beside her, Donovan grunted.

Ahead, the ocean came into focus. It was all dark-blue water, with enormous, white-topped waves.

In the distance, she spotted some rocky islands—long, narrow mountains pointing up like a predator's teeth.

"I can't...control the ship." She fought desperately to slow their descent.

"We can't—"

Whatever he was about to say was cut off.

They hit the water with a huge splash.

Metal crunched, and they were both tossed hard between the seats and harnesses.

The ship's momentum carried them toward the closest island, the rocky beach rushing closer and closer.

*Cren, they were going to hit the rocks.*

"Donovan." She reached for his hand.

His fingers closed on hers.

Then there was a massive crash, and then...nothing.

---

DONOVAN SWALLOWED A GROAN.

Damn, he hurt all over. It reminded him of his Space Corps Academy survival training sessions. The instructors had delighted in putting the recruits through hell. He shifted gingerly, and realized he was hanging upside down, his head throbbing.

He opened his eyes and blinked, every muscle tensing.

He was hanging upside down from a tree.

It only took seconds for him to take stock. A chill wind blew over him. He was tied to a leafless tree that had slick, black bark, and he was hanging from his ankles like a slab of meat.

His arms were free, his fingers numb. One of his eyes was swollen shut, and he felt the stickiness of drying blood on his face.

Careful to avoid drawing attention to himself, he looked around.

He was tied up at the edge of some rough, makeshift camp. A few men sat around a fire, all of them wearing ragged layers of clothes—torn fabric, furs.

They were on a rocky shore, the waves roughly lapping the beach. Light glinted off something in the distance. *Metal*. He sucked in a breath, taking in the ruins of their shuttle.

It was a crumpled, destroyed mess.

Damn, he was lucky he was still alive. His gut cramped. *Where was Airen?*

Panic was like acid in his throat. He didn't see her. Donovan wasn't used to panicking. God, *fuck*, had she made it? Had these assholes hurt her? His heart thundered. *Where was she?*

Suddenly, he realized the nearby conversation had stopped. He glanced over and saw the men looking his way.

A big one rose and sauntered over. His leather-and-fur boots crunched on the rocky ground. The man had rough, orange skin, almost reptilian looking. A coat made from some animal was wrapped around his big body.

"You're alive." The alien had a deep, rumbling voice like thunder.

"Yeah, feel like shit, though."

The alien smiled, showing teeth that looked like sharp, broken points. Up close, Donovan saw the man also had tattoos on his skin—rough, uneven ones. They hadn't been done by any artist or expert.

They looked like prison tattoos.

"My name is Crux. Welcome to Oblivion."

"We weren't meant to land here. We were shot down."

"Sorry to hear that." Crux grunted. "Anyone who ends up on Oblivion never gets off."

Well, Donovan had no plans to stay, but he wisely kept his mouth shut.

The alien pointed to the purple-blue sky. "They have a planetary security field. Lets ships in, but not out. Only way out is through the prison command base, where the wardens are." Crux smiled, showing jagged teeth. "The wardens don't let *anyone* off."

Donovan's stomach dropped. *Fuck.* "I wasn't alone—"

"Oh, we know."

The way the man drawled the words made Donovan's blood run cold. "Where is she?" *Be alive, Airen.*

"She's still breathing."

Donovan ground his teeth together. He knew he had

to play the game to get himself and Airen out of here alive. "So, you got any food you can share?"

The man eyed him for a second, then pulled out a giant knife.

Donovan tensed, then Crux reached up and sliced through the bindings at Donovan's ankles.

He hit the ground, pausing for a second to catch his breath. He ignored all the aches and pains rising up through his body. He rubbed his sore ankles, then rose, stretching his back.

"You look like a strong one. A good addition to our clan."

"Sounds good." Donovan forced his voice to stay even.

"We all look out for each other. Hunt, fight, survive. It's necessary in this place. Alone, you won't last very long."

Donovan nodded. Together, they moved toward the fire.

"My companion..." Donovan began.

Crux's lime-green eyes narrowed. "Women are good for one thing, friend." The alien's ugly grin made it clear what he thought that was. "I like them screaming and clawing under me."

Donovan barely restrained himself from knocking the man out. "She's mine."

"Not anymore," Crux said.

Donovan stiffened.

The alien laughed, and slapped Donovan's back, hard. "You still have a chance to claim her back."

"Oh?" *Keep your cool.*

"Yeah, in the hunt."

Donovan followed the man's gaze, and his heart swelled about three times its size. He spotted Airen in a small cage. She was crouched, naked, her fingers gripping the dark wooden bars. She glared at them.

He sucked in a breath. *She was alive.* The bastards had stripped her, but she was alive.

*Play the game.* Get Airen, then get the fuck away from here.

Donovan glanced up. He knew the Kantos would come. And he and Airen couldn't afford to be anywhere near the crash site when they did.

"Okay." He turned toward the fire. "What's the hunt?"

"Any females we find, we set them loose. Then we hunt 'em down." Crux laughed. "Whoever catches the prize gets to claim her. Then she's yours to fuck as you please."

Donovan breathed through his nose. *You can't kill him. Not yet.* "I'm so hungry I could eat a horse." He tried to keep his tone light.

"What's a horse?"

"Big animal on my planet."

"Well, we have food and drink. Come meet the others and rest up, so you can see if you can claim back your woman."

# CHAPTER TEN

Airen nursed her fury.

She was locked up, naked, and her captors were drinking and eating like they didn't have a care in the world.

And Donovan was there laughing with them. After that first long look, he hadn't even glanced her way once.

A cold wind rushed over her and she shivered. She was cold, naked, and hungry. She still had some aches and fading bruises from the crash, but thankfully, by some stroke of luck, she wasn't badly injured. Her helian was healing the worst of her minor scrapes.

She shivered again. She could give herself her armor, but she didn't want to give her helian abilities away to her captors.

She dragged in a deep breath. Donovan was clearly gaining the criminals' trust, but she was still mad at the situation. She didn't like being naked, exposed. She didn't remember much from the crash, just waking up to rough hands tearing her clothes off. She'd been groggy and disoriented, and thankfully her helian had dissolved her armor before the criminals had found them.

Before she could fight back, she'd been stuffed in a cage.

When she'd come to again, she'd seen Donovan hanging from a tree. She bit her lip. At first, she'd thought he was dead, and it had hurt. Her chest had felt ripped open. She'd been damn glad when he'd woken up.

Airen had growing feelings for the stubborn, tough Terran. Donovan was honorable, and didn't hide how much he admired and desired her. She squeezed her eyes closed, a mix of emotion churning in her belly. Falling for Donovan was almost scarier than Oblivion.

*You'd better remember he doesn't believe in the long-term, Airen, and focus on getting off this prison planet alive.*

She glanced up at the sky. The distant sun was lowering toward the watery horizon, and the temperature was already dropping. She guessed Donovan was waiting for the right moment to make a move.

She counted the group of criminals. There were too many of them. Even if she and Donovan were free and had weapons, the men would still overpower them.

The criminals' voices rose, getting louder and more ribald. She tensed. Something was going on. They were standing now, nudging each other and glancing her way. One grabbed his crotch, threw his head back, and howled at the sky.

She sensed the hyped-up energy, and she watched as they gathered in a crowd at the edge of the jungle. The trees on this planet lacked color; all grays, blacks, and dark browns.

Donovan looked her way and their gazes locked. She saw the determined glint in his eyes, and he gave her a small nod.

Two men broke away from the crowd, lumbering in her direction. Their big frames were covered in furs.

"Hope you can run, female," one drawled.

The other criminal laughed.

They opened the cage, and one reached in and yanked her out.

She ignored the blatant way they looked at her naked body. She was an Eon warrior and she wasn't afraid.

She fought not to look over their shoulders at Donovan. She reminded herself she wasn't alone.

"I want to win this one," the other man drawled, his ugly face alight. "She's skinny, but she needs breaking."

*Lovely.* "Win?" she said in a bored tone.

"Yeah, it's time for the hunt." The big one dragged her across the rocky ground to the edge of the jungle. The jagged stones pricked her bare feet.

The men in the crowd jumped and rocked. Preparing for something.

"The rules are simple," the alien said. "You run, and whoever catches you, claims you."

She stiffened. She could take him down, but even with Donovan's help, she couldn't take them all down.

The alien leaned closer, his fetid breath washing over her face. "And your new owner can do whatever he wants to you." He reached out and cupped her breast.

She knocked his arm away, and when he swung to slap her, she dodged.

*Don't fight him. Don't show your skills. Not yet.* If they chased her, she could pick them off one by one in the trees.

And Donovan would come for her.

The alien growled. "This should be fun." He shoved her. "Now run."

Airen shot one last look toward the crowd, then she sprinted into the jungle.

Dark leaves slapped at her, and the wind picked up. She ran through the trees and pushed thick vines out of her way. She spotted a trailing vine lying across the path, short spikes tipped with noxious-looking, neon-green fluid. She leaped over it.

She had to get far enough away so that she could form her armor. Not yet, because they might be watching her. She'd seen the battered binocs resting on the alien's belt.

It didn't help that night was falling, the shadows under the trees growing.

A horn sounded—long and deep. Then she heard shouts and whistles in the distance.

Her mouth firmed. Her "hunters" were coming.

Airen sprinted hard. Suddenly, her leg went down through a hole in the ground. It was filled with slushy brown water and full of rotting leaves.

*Ugh.* Her foot was stuck in some mud at the bottom and she yanked, pulling it out.

She was losing time.

She took off again, keeping one eye on the ground to make sure she didn't fall in any other holes.

She heard a noise. A twig snapping. She swiveled and frowned. She saw nothing through the leaves. Surely none of the criminals had caught up with her yet, but they did have the advantage of knowing the terrain better than she did.

*Keep moving.* She turned and had taken two steps when she was tackled from behind.

She hit the ground hard, a heavy body on top of her. She smelled rancid breath and rank body odor.

"You're mine now, girly."

---

DONOVAN'S HEART was pumping as he ran hard. He leaped over a fallen log of black, twisted wood.

Nearby, he heard the shouts of the other criminals. They were fanning out, crashing through the vegetation like a pack of wolves.

*Where the hell was Airen?*

He slapped through some glowing vines. Then he heard the sounds of a struggle. He cocked his head. *To the right.* He plowed into the trees, picking up speed.

He broke out of the vegetation and saw Airen wrestling with a man in ragged clothes. The man growled, showing a mouth with no teeth.

Suddenly, Airen shoved him off her and rose. Her armor formed, scales flowing up over her slim body.

The criminal stared at her, face shocked, and made a choked sound. He stumbled to his feet.

She formed a short sword on her arm and it glowed with a green edge.

The criminal pulled a large, jagged blade off his belt. It looked like it was made of scavenged metal.

He rushed her.

Airen cut him down with one swipe.

"You all right?" Donovan jogged over to her.

She nodded.

He took a second to yank her close and pressed his face to her hair. Her arms clamped around him.

"Can we get out of here?" she said.

"Good idea. I keep expecting the Kantos to arrive."

Green-black eyes met his. "They won't be far away."

Then, because he needed it, needed to touch her and reassure himself that she was okay, he pulled her even closer. His lips touched hers, a gentle, searching kiss. "I'm sorry about what those assholes did to you."

"I'm fine now." She leaned into him for a second, reaching up to stroke his swollen eye. "When I saw you in that tree, I thought you were dead."

"I'm pretty hard to kill."

She let out a choked laugh. "We need to go."

Donovan reluctantly released her and went down on one knee. He grabbed the criminal's sword. It was poorly made, the weight all wrong, but it was better than nothing.

With Airen by his side, they took off running. Shouts echoed not too far away.

All of a sudden, a body dropped from a tree. It hit Donovan, and they crashed to the ground. His attacker's heavy weight knocked the air out of him.

*Fuck, that hurt.* He wheezed.

Gasping, he squirmed beneath his attacker, turning to get a glimpse of the criminal on top of him—a younger male, wiry and strong, with reptilian eyes that had elongated pupils.

Suddenly, the criminal rolled off Donovan and sprang at Airen.

Damn, he moved fast.

She kicked him and they fought. They traded several blows and kicks, but the criminal was so quick, most of Airen's blows hit air. The criminal swiped out with a knife he pulled out of nowhere. Airen spun and slashed with her sword.

The man leaped back, then moved again, blindingly fast.

Donovan pushed up, sucking in air and strode closer.

The criminal's knife hit Airen's armor. Donovan's heart thumped, but her armor protected her. She dodged to the side.

Donovan got close, and with a roar, he swung his sword, but the criminal was gone like smoke.

*Fuck.* The asshole was too quick.

The criminal danced around, taunting them. He darted toward a tree and pushed off of it. He sprinted toward Airen again.

She didn't move, her face set, her sword held up.

"You'll never catch me." The criminal had a high-pitched voice. "I'll claim you, female, and kill your man and drink his blood." He flicked out a forked tongue.

Airen stayed still, watching the man with a laser-like gaze.

He rushed at her.

Her sword flashed. She impaled the man on her blade.

He glanced down in disbelief at the sword through his gut, then he choked, blood running out of his mouth. She pulled the sword free and the man collapsed to the ground.

"You talk too much," she said.

"Damn, you're something, Second Commander."

She looked at Donovan, and he took in the fierce lines of her face. He wanted her. Desperately.

She smiled at him.

Then they heard a loud, baying cry, followed by hoots and hollers. The criminals were close.

*Fuck.* "They're coming."

"All of them," she said. "We can't take them all down." She frowned. "There are too many."

*Damn. Damn. Damn.* He met her gaze. "I need you to trust me."

She hesitated a second, then she nodded.

"Take your armor off. You need to let me claim you."

Her eyes flared bright turquoise.

"We can't give away your armor or skills just yet." He strode right up to her. "Let me protect you, Airen. Play the game, and we'll escape as soon as we can."

She drew in a harsh breath, then she nodded.

He cupped her cheek. He knew this was hard for his proud warrior. To make herself vulnerable, put herself in his hands.

Her scales flickered away, folding back until she was naked.

"I know it's not the time," he said. "But you are so damn beautiful, Airen."

She swallowed.

Donovan crouched and swiped his fingers through the dead criminal's blood. When he rose, he streaked some across her cheek. She didn't flinch, just lifted her chin. He moved his hands lower, and smeared blood across her upper chest. His hand brushed against her breast and they both sucked in a breath.

Then they heard the shouts. The criminals were almost there.

"Kneel, Airen."

She quivered, then dropped to her knees at his feet.

Shit, he hated this.

Crux and the others broke out of the trees.

Their gazes went straight to Airen and Donovan, then flicked to the dead criminal sprawled on the ground.

Donovan tangled his hand in Airen's hair, tilting her face up.

"I claim her. She's mine."

# CHAPTER ELEVEN

Night had fallen and Airen sat on her knees, still naked, pressed against Donovan's legs.

They were back at the criminals' camp, all sitting around the fire.

She listened to the laughter and deep voices. Even though she wasn't wearing any clothes, the fire and proximity to Donovan were keeping her warm.

The criminals sat around eating and drinking some noxious beverage that they brewed from tree roots. They were all half drunk, and a few of them had passed out. She'd listened to them brag about the horrid crimes they'd committed in order to be sent to Oblivion.

"You gonna fuck your toy, new guy?" a man called out. "We'd enjoy the show."

Donovan glared at the man, as he'd been doing every time someone looked her way.

She fought back a smile. She liked him taking care of her. *Cren.* She'd been protecting herself a long time, but this Terran was getting under her skin.

Making her feel so much.

She eyed the harsh, desperate men around them. She knew they'd keep pushing him, unless she and Donovan gave them something.

She pressed closer to him and moved between his spread legs. She felt his muscles tense.

His gaze was on her now, the firelight turning his eyes a vibrant orange-gold. He cupped her jaw, and she nuzzled into his palm.

He had such strong hands.

Then he hauled her into his lap and wrapped an arm around her. She pressed her face against his neck. Even after everything they'd been through, he still smelled good. All man.

She moved her mouth to his ear and nipped his earlobe. His fingers stroked her hip. She saw his big hand on her. How dark it was against her paler skin.

She moved her mouth higher and whispered. "Are the rest of them ever going to pass out?"

"Fuck, I hope so," he murmured.

"We need to get out of here." She knew the Kantos would come. They were running out of time.

"Donovan, my friend," Crux called out. "If you want some privacy with your female, you're welcome to use the shelters." The alien jerked his head.

A few ragged tents made of furs and hides had been set up near the trees.

Donovan nodded and rose, lifting Airen in his arms.

Her heart gave a little thump. She liked him carrying her. Way too much.

He strode across the ground and ducked into the tent. He set her down and then fiddled with a small container filled with oil. He lit it, and golden light filled the makeshift tent.

He touched her shoulder. "How are you doing?"

"I'm okay."

He nodded, but he didn't look happy. "I want to beat each of those assholes to a pulp every time they look at you."

She cupped his cheek. "Right now, we need to focus on getting out of here."

"Crux told me more about Oblivion's planetary security net. To get through it, we need to head to the prison command. From what I gather, it's not on this island, and he said the place is packed with wardens. All trained to kill unruly inmates."

She blew out a breath. She'd known it wouldn't be easy. "I hope Malax and the *Rengard* can find us."

The shuttle had a tracking beacon in it, but she knew that both of them were aware that there was slim hope of the warriors finding them. The wormhole had dumped them too far away.

"Fucking Kantos," Donovan said.

"So." Airen straightened. "We get away from your new friends, and find the location of the prison command."

"That's our plan." He pulled her close, and she wrapped her arms around him.

"I'm glad I'm with you," she said quietly. "And not alone."

"Damn, me too, Airen."

They looked at each other, the light flickering over their faces. And then she moved, leaning up until her lips touched his.

He kissed her, and only took seconds to deepen the kiss, taking her mouth hungrily. Her hands slid over his short hair and she moaned. By the warriors, he tasted so good, and felt even better. Desire was a hot, burning fire inside her.

It felt like seconds, and it felt like forever, but finally, she reluctantly broke the kiss.

Panting, he pressed his forehead to hers. "You obliterate my control, Airen. Any time I touch you, it's just gone."

She smiled. "I like knowing that."

His answering smile was wide and white. "I bet you do."

Suddenly, bright lights speared through the cracks of the tent. Shouts echoed outside.

The chaos was followed by the unmistakable sound of laser fire.

"Fuck," Donovan bit out.

They both leaped up and Airen formed her armor, instantly feeling much less vulnerable.

Donovan shifted a flap of the tent, and through the opening, she spotted a Kantos ship in the sky. It fired at the criminals, who scattered across the camp.

A moment later, several Kantos soldiers skittered out of the trees and into view.

"We need to move," she said.

Donovan rummaged through the gear in the tent, and grabbed a knife and a rusted sword. He also threw some food and drink in a leather bag and swung it onto his shoulder.

He turned and slashed at the furs at the back of the tent. They both pushed out of the slit and ran outside. They sprinted toward the trees.

Lights hit them.

*Cren.*

Laser fire cut up the ground, moving toward them. Airen dived on Donovan, shielding him.

Dirt and rocks flew around them, and a second later, a sharp burn sliced across her back and she cried out.

"Airen!"

Wincing, she rolled off him. The pain made it impossible to talk.

Donovan lifted her and she fought off the agony. She had to stay conscious. He started running, and then, they were in the trees.

Airen dragged in a breath, her vision blurring. *Don't pass out and don't vomit.*

Donovan set her down against a tree trunk.

"Baby, let me—" He touched her shoulder, trying to look at her back.

"O-kay. Helian...stopping pain. Healing."

The air shuddered out of him. "You're sure?"

She managed a nod.

"Can you move?"

She knew that she didn't have a choice. She nodded again.

He helped her up, keeping an arm around her, careful not to bump her laser burn.

Then they set off running.

---

DONOVAN GROUND HIS TEETH TOGETHER, scanning the jungle as they ran.

Airen had fucking taken a hit to protect him. For a blinding second, he'd been sure that she was dead. Her weight had been on him, her body lax.

He glanced down at her. She was looking stronger and she seemed fine, but his body was still on edge.

He heard shouts and screams, and the sound of fighting. The criminals were fighting back, and the Kantos ship still hovered over the camp.

Now, he and Airen needed to put as much distance between them and the Kantos as they could, and then find somewhere safe to hole up.

The sound of heavy bodies crashing through the trees reached them. *Dammit.*

*You cannot escape us, Eon female.*

A shiver ran down Donovan's neck. An elite Kantos. Only they had the ability to speak telepathically in other people's heads.

Airen cursed. "Faster."

They picked up speed.

*We will capture you.*

"You can try," she muttered.

A piercing, buzzing noise cut through the night.

With a sharp cry, Airen dropped to her knees, her hands clasped over her ears. Her face contorted.

"Airen?"

"It...hurts," she moaned.

Donovan looked around and realized the noise was worse for her. It was some weapon designed to mess with an Eon warrior's acute hearing.

A second later, two Kantos appeared, skittering on their four legs. One was the elite—a little taller and paler than the other soldier.

Donovan stepped in front of Airen and lifted his sword. Damn, he wished he had a better weapon.

The Kantos soldier rushed forward, his arms slicing through the air.

Donovan ducked, swiveled, then dropped to his knees. He saw those four sharp legs and he chopped out at one, aiming for a joint. He knew all the weak spots on a Kantos soldier's body.

The Kantos teetered. As it struggled for balance, Donovan leaped up and kicked it. As soon as it hit the ground, he drove his sword down into its chest.

There was a cracking sound, as metal met the hard shell of the Kantos' body. Grunting, Donovan forced his sword in.

Green blood leaked out of the alien's chest, and a second later, it went still.

Airen was still on the ground, trying to get up, but it was clear that the agony was keeping her down. Her hands were pressed to her ears.

Donovan turned, and spotted the device clutched by the elite. With a growl, he strode toward the alien.

The elite swung an arm, and Donovan danced back.

"Come on, asshole."

*Your taunts mean nothing to me, Terran. You are weak and insignificant.*

Donovan charged in and swung his sword. It sliced across the elite's hard shell without injuring the Kantos.

*I will kill you, then take what I came for.*

"You know, I'm sick to death of everyone thinking Airen is a thing. Treating her like a commodity. Fuck you. She's Airen Kann-Felis, Eon warrior and second commander of the *Rengard*. She'll cut you up into tiny pieces, and I'll enjoy watching her do it."

With a vicious swing, Donovan cut his sword through the air and hit the device. It smashed.

Airen shook her head and rose. Blood was leaking out of one of her ears. Her sword formed on her arm, contained fury on her face. She stalked toward the elite.

The Kantos skittered back a step.

*You will never—*

Airen swung her sword. She tore into the Kantos, and Donovan jumped in as well, attacking from the side.

The alien went down under their brutal blows.

When the elite was dead, Airen stepped back, her chest heaving.

Donovan eyed her carefully. "Feel better?"

She tossed her tangled hair back. "I do."

"Good."

A faint smile curled her lips. "Not bad for a weak, insignificant Terran."

He snorted, cleaning his sword off on a bush. "The

weakest people are always the ones who have to belittle you and exaggerate their own abilities."

She nodded. "And the strongest are the ones who'd stand by your side and never let you down."

*Damn.* Donovan felt her words deep in his gut.

All of a sudden, he heard shouts, followed by a sharp whistle that echoed behind them in the trees.

*Dammit.* Crux and his gang were coming.

"We're going to find you, new guy." Crux's bellow echoed through the trees. "We're going to take your woman. We hear she's worth a lot of credits and a ride off this rock."

"Fucking fuck." The Kantos had recruited Crux and his criminals. "We need to move."

She nodded.

Together, they jogged into the vegetation.

"Let's keep going," she said. "The more distance we can put between us and the criminals, the better."

They kept running, but the shouts never went away. The criminals knew the land better than them, and they were not going to let them go.

The island terrain narrowed, and he saw moonlight glinting off the ocean on either side. They moved up a hill, and when they looked back, moonlight speared down through the trees. He saw the crowd of criminals, many of them holding burning torches above their heads.

They were like a pack of rabid dogs.

He and Airen jogged down the hill. They ran out of the trees and stumbled to a halt.

"Shit."

A massive, wide waterfall blocked their way. It was

full of smooth, small platforms of rock, filled with pools of steaming water.

The water glowed in bright greens and yellows, caused by whatever minerals were in the water. And it was clearly hot. Steam rose off the pools.

Donovan's jaw tightened. "How the hell are we going to get past this?"

# CHAPTER TWELVE

Airen's pain was finally fading, but her ears still throbbed. Her head felt like it was caught in a hard vise, and her helian was working overtime to heal up the last of the damage.

"There's high geothermal activity here," she said.

Behind them, the shouts and cries were getting closer.

"We need to get across," Donovan said.

They both knew the criminals' blood lust was up. And there could be more Kantos anywhere around them in the jungle.

Airen studied the waterfall and pools. Black stone edged the pools, and in places, there were some large, flat stepping stones.

She nodded. "Let's go." She started across the rock, holding her arms out for balance.

Donovan moved in behind her.

"How hot is this water?" he asked.

"Hot. Don't fall."

As they made their way across, she glanced ahead. A solid wall of rock barred their way, and her gut cramped. They'd have to climb—

No, wait. There was a cave.

*Cren*, she hoped it led somewhere.

"Airen, faster," Donovan said.

She picked up speed. To her left in a pool, she saw a snake-like creature appear, swimming lazily. It disappeared down into the cloudy, glowing, green-and-yellow-tinged water.

Wild shouts broke out behind them, and when she glanced back, she saw the criminals at the edge of the jungle, pointing at them.

The first one started across the rocks after them.

It wasn't long before several criminals were crossing the pools in a single line.

Airen paused and climbed up to a higher pool. The rocks were hot to touch.

"Gonna kill you, traitor," a criminal yelled. "Then I'm gonna claim that female, have some fun with her, then sell her."

Donovan turned and pulled out a knife. He gripped the hilt, looked down, then threw it.

The blade slammed into the criminal's neck and the man teetered, his arms waving madly. He fell into a pool with a splash.

He came up thrashing in the water, his screams making them all freeze. Airen watched as his skin started to melt off his bones. She winced.

Donovan cursed and turned. "Keep going. And don't fall."

She carefully placed her feet, and drew in a steadying breath. They kept moving.

Suddenly, there was a whistle of sound.

A long, wooden arrow flew past them, its sharp end hitting the rock. It rebounded off the stone and landed in the water with a splash, sizzling as it melted.

"What the hell?" Donovan barked.

Airen glanced back. A tall, pale-skinned alien held some sort of crossbow.

"Go, go, go," Donovan yelled.

She tried to move faster, but they couldn't go too fast, or they'd risk falling into the water.

Two more arrows flew past. Airen crouched down, and saw Donovan do the same. The bolts hit the water with a dangerous splash.

Close. *Too close.*

"Go ahead of me," she said.

"No."

"Donovan—"

"You're not going to be my damn shield, Airen. Let's just get across, as fast as we can."

*Stubborn Terran.* She moved into a crouch and kept moving. The cave mouth was getting closer.

They were almost there.

She heard the whistle of another arrow, then Donovan grunted.

*No!* She spun. She saw him over-balancing.

Airen lunged and caught his arm. She gritted her teeth, holding him tightly so they both didn't topple into the geothermal pool.

"Donovan." She saw the ugly point of the arrow spearing out his chest. *Cren.*

"Keep...moving." His voice was drenched with pain.

"Donovan—"

"Move, Airen."

With little choice, she kept holding him and they shuffled closer to the cave.

They reached a row of stepping stones, and she carefully stepped out on one. They crossed over them, and by the time they reached the other side, Donovan's face was covered in sweat.

They'd made it across the pools. *Finally.* She turned and formed a blaster with her helian. She fired several energy blasts.

Some criminals fell, while others crouched low to avoid the shots.

She fired again, this time, right into one of the pools. Boiling-hot water splashed up, and more criminals screamed.

Donovan slumped against the wall, his chest heaving. Blood streamed down his chest. She saw the rest of the arrow protruding out of his back. The pain had to be horrible.

"Let me—"

"We can't stop yet," he said.

She knew he was right, but she hated knowing that he was hurt and injured. That he was in so much pain.

Reaching behind him, she snapped the back of the arrow off. Even that made him groan. It was all she could do for now. She slid her arm around him and they started into the cave.

It was long and twisting, and Airen formed a light on her armor. The walls gleamed with a rainbow sheen of light. Some sort of luminescent organisms, she guessed.

"Come on." She kept her tone upbeat. "We'll find somewhere to hide and get you patched up."

He grunted. In the low light, she saw that his dark skin had taken on an unhealthy sheen.

They shuffled through the tunnel. The glimmering walls might have been pretty, but she was too worried to really notice. A faint light glowed at the end of the tunnel, and her adrenaline spiked. "We're almost out of the cave, Donovan."

Behind them, she heard the criminals' voices echo off the walls. *Cren!* They were inside the cave.

Airen and Donovan stumbled out into faint early-morning light. A wall of trees greeted them.

They needed to hide. *Now.*

Stumbling, they hurried into the trees. They were moving up a gentle slope. She heard Donovan try to stifle a groan of pain. Airen scanned ahead, searching for any place where they could hole up.

Then the trees ended. Her stomach plummeted.

She arched her head up, looking at the sheer walls of black rock rising up ahead of them. The cave had led them through one rocky mountain and led them straight to a second one. This one was even higher and more forbidding.

That was it. Despair hit her like a drowning wave. There was nowhere to go. No way to get through.

Nowhere to hide.

They'd reached a dead end.

DONOVAN FOUGHT hard to stay conscious. Blood flowed down his chest and back freely. He stared at the rock wall, grinding his teeth together.

"Climb," he bit out.

Airen spun. "What?"

"Climb the cliff." He had no doubt she could do it. "I'll do whatever I can to hold them off you."

Her eyes flashed a brilliant turquoise. "And leave you to face them, to be killed, so I can run like a coward?"

*Stubborn woman.* "The Kantos want *you.* Those criminals will hurt you and hand you over without a second thought. I *won't* let that happen."

"*We* won't let it. I won't leave you, Donovan." Her voice lowered. "I can't."

*Dammit to hell.*

Voices echoed from the cave. Strange, the criminals seemed to be hanging back. Probably planning their attack.

And more Kantos wouldn't be far behind.

"Please, Airen." He needed her safe.

She slid a firm arm around him. "Not. Leaving."

"Stubborn." The word was ripe with frustration.

She formed her blaster again and she focused, going into full warrior mode.

Donovan wanted to fight the incoming criminals, but his strength was draining out of him. He drew in a shuddering breath. The best he could do now was stay out of her way.

Down the slope, he saw the first criminals appear at

the cave mouth. They picked up speed, running into the trees.

One appeared, lifting his crossbow. He fired. The projectiles hit the rock wall just above Airen and Donovan's heads.

Airen fired her blaster, a bolt of green energy forcing the criminals to duck. More bodies stepped out of the cave.

*Damn.* They'd charge before too long.

Donovan gritted his teeth. He had no way to keep Airen safe.

With wild cries, more criminals ran out of the cave. They were motivated by the promise of a chance to get off this prison planet. Airen fired again.

A stocky criminal broke from the trees, launching at them with a huge sword in his hands. Airen's weapon morphed, changing into a sword. She spun, her blade slamming against the criminal's. With a roar, the man swung, and got in a lucky hit. His blade cut across Airen's stomach, opening up a long, thin line across her armor and skin.

She pressed her hand to the bleeding wound.

Donovan pushed away from the wall, and his knees threatened to go out from under him. He had to help her.

Suddenly, spears rained down from the sky.

The criminals cried out, several going down under the spears, slamming into the dirt.

Donovan looked up.

"*Cren,*" Airen breathed.

Bodies were running down the rock wall, attached to

ropes behind them. Several held bows, while others clutched spears.

They were all women clad in leather.

Donovan blinked, his vision blurring.

The women hit the ground, and let out a warbling, wild, battle cry. They rushed at the criminals.

The men turned and ran back into the cave.

There were several wounded criminals trying to drag themselves away, but the female warriors dispatched them quickly and dispassionately.

As the women turned, Airen shifted closer to Donovan.

He had to lean on her to stay upright.

Two warriors stepped forward. One was shorter and curvier, with brown skin and black hair in a mass of curls. The other was tall, flat-chested, and toned. Her brown hair was clipped short around her skull. Both women's cool gazes studied them.

The curvy one looked at Airen. "Are you all right?"

Airen nodded. "Thank you for your assistance."

The woman flicked an unreadable glance at Donovan, then looked back at Airen.

"My name is Sanya." The woman wore tight leather trousers and a sleeveless vest that displayed her impressive cleavage. "You are welcome into our sanctuary."

"Thank you," Airen replied.

"Your...friend is not."

Airen stiffened. "I'm not going—"

"Go with them," he said.

She glared at Sanya. "He's with me."

The woman gave a violent shake of her head. "No men."

"What?" Airen demanded. "Why?"

"Most of our residents escaped from those animals." She stabbed a finger at the cave. "Or others like them."

*Fuck.* Donovan wavered. He wasn't going to be able to stay on his feet much longer. Pain was a massive throb through his torso, the arrow still embedded in his skin. But as long as Airen was safe, he didn't care.

"Take her," he said.

"No." Airen straightened. "Donovan is *nothing* like those men." She pressed closer to him. "He's mine." She lifted her head, her gaze boring into his.

He felt warmth move through his chest, and tried to fight it down. He'd never, ever wanted a woman to be his, but this Eon warrior made him feel so damn much.

"Don't be stubborn," he said. "I want you to be safe."

"Donovan—"

At that moment, his body gave up, and he collapsed.

Airen cried out, catching most of his weight, and lowering him to the ground. She laid him on his side. "Donovan."

"Sorry...Airen." His own labored breathing echoed in his ears.

"Don't you do this, Terran." Her hands on his chest. "I *won't* let you die on me."

He couldn't talk anymore, couldn't make his lips form any words. He lifted a shaky hand and she grabbed it.

He saw her perfectly shaped lips moving.

*She'd be okay.* These warriors would help her.

Then the blackness sucked him under.

## CHAPTER THIRTEEN

F ear pounded through Airen, amplified by her helian.

She met Sanya's gaze. The woman studied her with a hard edge. This was a woman used to making tough decisions.

"He's earned my loyalty," Airen said. "Like I guess you've earned the loyalty of your warriors."

The leader paused for a second. "He was willing to risk himself for you to survive."

"That's the kind of man he is." Airen couldn't stop herself stroking Donovan's face.

"Come," Sanya said. "Bring him."

"Sanya," the tall warrior objected.

The leader held up her hand. "It is my word, Tira."

The warrior stepped back, but she didn't look happy.

"You'll help us?" Airen asked, hope threading through her.

Sanya nodded.

Airen stayed close to Donovan. She was unsure how

she'd get him up the steep cliff walls. His breathing was so labored, and her stomach clutched. He was badly injured.

"He likely won't survive," Tira said blandly. "The bacteria here is dangerous. Most injuries result in infections that are fatal."

Airen stiffened. "He's a fighter. And stubborn."

"Wylo, Danice," the leader called out.

A pair of female warriors knelt beside Donovan and unfolded a large bundle of leather. It was a makeshift stretcher. They loaded Donovan onto it and Airen rose.

Suddenly, there was a rumbling in the rock wall and she swung around. She watched as a square of the rock moved inward.

*Amazing.* Some sort of doorway.

Inside was a tunnel, and she spotted more leather-clad women waiting for them.

The leader waved everybody inside. Ahead, Airen found hewn steps leading upward. They climbed for what felt like a very long time. Finally, they reached the top, and there was a large, open area filled with women. Windows were cut into the rock, and she caught glimpses of ocean and island.

It looked like the inside of a castle.

Women sat around watching them. These residents weren't warriors. Most wore long skirts and dresses. Several children laughed, running past them.

They walked through the open area and down a long, internal hall. It was lit by torches spaced along the wall. The warriors carried Donovan into a room with one narrow window.

There was a bed on the ground. No frame, just some sort of leather mattress stuffed with something and covered in furs.

The warriors set Donovan down on it. He rested on his side, his horrible wound making Airen's belly clench to a hard point.

"I will send the healer," Sanya said.

"Thank you," Airen said. "I truly appreciate your help."

The woman nodded. "We will always aid a woman in need." Her gaze drifted down Airen's armor. "And a fellow warrior."

"My name is Airen Kann-Felis. I am an Eon warrior."

Sanya cocked her head, her curls sliding over her shoulders. "I've heard of your species. And your man?"

*Her man.* Airen liked the sound of that. "He's Terran, from the planet Earth."

"I've not heard of it."

"They're recent allies of the Eon. We share an enemy. The Kantos."

Sanya's dark eyes flared.

"You know the Kantos?" Airen asked carefully.

"Yes." The warrior leader turned her head and pulled in a ragged breath. "The insects destroyed my planet."

Airen froze.

"They killed billions. Just thousands of us were left, refugees, mostly females. We had nothing, so we turned to raiding." She gave a humorless smile. "That's how I ended up here."

"I'm so sorry. Donovan's planet is also under attack by the Kantos. He and my people are trying to defeat them." Airen paused. "There are Kantos here on Oblivion. They're after me."

Sanya gave a curt nod. "You are safe here. Our fortress is impregnable and we know how to defend it. I'll send the healer, and I hope your man recovers. Any enemy of the Kantos is a friend of mine."

After Sanya had left, Airen studied the sparse room for a moment, then sat down beside Donovan. She eyed the ugly arrow head still embedded in his skin. She needed to get it out, and she wished she had havv. The healing bio-organisms would guarantee his recovery.

There was a soft knock at the door.

"Come in," Airen called out.

A woman entered. Long, tangled, blonde hair fell over her face, and ragged skirts fell around her thin body. She looked nervously at Airen, clutching a basket to her chest.

Airen noticed horrible scars on one side of the woman's face. Someone had hurt this woman terribly.

The healer glanced at Donovan, and she looked scared. She swallowed rapidly.

Airen felt a surge of anger, suspecting she knew how the woman had gotten the scars, and who had hurt her.

The woman detected Airen's emotions and bobbled the basket.

"You're the healer?" Airen asked, keeping her voice low and calm.

The woman nodded.

"I'm Airen. This is Donovan. He's badly hurt."

The woman steeled herself and came forward. She

knelt beside the bed and set the basket down. It was filled with cloths, bottles, and jars.

She gestured to the arrow stuck in Donovan's torso.

"You want me to remove it?"

The woman nodded.

Up close, Airen saw more scarring around the woman's throat, and figured she either couldn't talk due to her injury, or the trauma that had accompanied it.

Airen looked at Donovan, reached down and wrapped her hand around the small amount of the arrow protruding from his back. "I'm sorry, Donovan."

With one quick movement, she pulled it out, and even unconscious, he jerked.

*I'm so sorry.* She touched his shoulder. "Shh."

Blood gushed from the wound. The healer hesitated, then she got to work. She grabbed some wadded fabric and pressed it to the injury. Next, she pulled out some pungent pastes and poultices.

Airen shoved the top of Donovan's suit down to his waist. The woman got to work, and soon seemed to forget that she was working on a man.

Finally, the woman sat back.

"Will he be okay?" Airen asked.

The healer shrugged. Then she rose, set a jar of poultice down beside the bed. With a bow of her head, she left.

Airen held Donovan's hand. She felt so helpless. If they were on the *Rengard*, Thane would heal him in an instant. If he was an Eon warrior, his helian would save him.

She lay down beside him on his uninjured side and pressed her face to his chest. "Fight, Donovan. Please."

Minutes later, another knock sounded. The door cracked open, and the healer reappeared. Several female warriors entered behind her.

Airen sat up and watched, as they carried a small wooden tub in, followed by several jugs of steaming water. The warriors set the tub down and filled it.

The healer moved toward Airen and set down a parcel. It contained clothes, soap, and food.

Gently, Airen touched the woman's arm. "Thank you. For everything."

That earned her a tiny smile from the healer, and then the woman left, the warriors following her out.

Once she was alone, Airen dipped a cloth into the warm water. She moved back and wiped down Donovan's chest and back, cleaning the blood away. She dipped the cloth again and wiped his face, careful of the swelling around his eye. Her poor Terran was more than a little battered. Her own body had a few aches and pains, but her helian was already hard at work healing her. Grabbing a small bladder of water, she dribbled some into his mouth.

She stood, commanding her helian armor to retract. It flickered away, and then she moved to the tub. The thin cut on her stomach was already healing.

It would be nice to be clean.

She sat in the tub, using the soap the healer had left to clean herself. It smelled of wildflowers and herbs.

When she got out, she dried herself with a cloth, and then pulled on the leather trousers and vest-like top that the healer left. The vest pushed her breasts up and showed a lot more cleavage than she was used to. Her nose wrinkled. Definitely not Eon warrior regulation.

"You need to heal, Donovan, and check out my new outfit." She knew he'd have something to say about it.

But instead, his chest rose and fell too fast, his eyes closed. His wound was an ugly gash against his dark skin, and Airen bit her lip.

She forced herself to eat a few bites of the food—crackers, bread, berries, and some sort of dried meat—but her appetite was next to nothing.

Finally, she moved back to the bed and settled down beside him. By Eschar's embrace, she hated feeling so completely useless. She stroked Donovan's short hair. This man who'd come to mean so much to her in such a short time.

"Get better, Donovan." *Please.*

---

AIREN STIRRED. She heard a deep groan and felt movement.

*Donovan.*

She shook off sleep, and realized it was pitch black in the room. Night had fallen, and they'd dozed most of the day away.

She found the lamp she'd spotted earlier and lit it.

When she turned, she saw Donovan twisting restlessly on the furs. Sweat covered his skin, and his wound was red and inflamed.

Her heart squeezed. *No.* It was infected.

She reached for the poultice the healer had left. She quickly applied more, then dipped the cloth in the now-cool water. She squeezed it out and then wiped down his face.

"I'm here. You're not alone." She kept wiping him down to cool him.

He seemed calmer when she spoke and touched him.

"No one's ever cared for me like this when I've been sick or injured." She swallowed a lump. "I wish that I'd had someone who cared."

She went on talking, telling him about growing up alone, unwanted.

*Cren.* These were old hurts that she never let herself think about anymore. Now, she was an Eon warrior. She'd found her place, a place where she belonged.

Donovan groaned.

*Oh, by the warriors.* The wound was so bad, his breathing shallow. She said a small word to the warrior Eschar, praying for his healing.

Airen realized that the way Donovan looked at her... Maybe she'd been missing something from her life for all this time.

Passion. A connection to one special person. Maybe it was worth the risk?

She listened to his breathing rattle and he thrashed again.

"Donovan." She leaned over him and pressed her forehead to his. She knew in her heart that he was dying.

And there wasn't a thing that she could do about it.

For the first time in years, she felt tears well in her eyes. They slid down her cheeks.

"I don't want you to die. I want you to kiss me again, to look at me that way you do. With desire, admiration. No one's ever looked at me quite like that. And you make me laugh." She rubbed her cheek against his. "No one makes me laugh like you do."

He went still, his chest barely moving. She was losing him.

Airen bit her lip and held his big hand, clutching it to her chest.

"I'm sorry, Donovan. I'd do anything to heal you."

Her helian throbbed, grieving with her.

Warmth flowed from her symbiont, and coalesced in her chest, burning hot. She felt movement and when she opened her eyes, she gasped.

Black scales were flowing from her helian and across to Donovan. *By the warriors.*

The scales covered half of his naked chest, over his wound. She swallowed. Only mates could share armor. Her helian had recognized Donovan as her mate.

She felt a pulse through her helian, and watched as his breathing eased. *Her helian was healing him.*

Relief filled her, and she lay down beside him, hand over his heart. She felt his heart beating stronger.

Then worry nipped at her. Donovan had made it clear that he didn't believe in love, or long-term relationships, and definitely did not want a mate.

She worried her lip. She couldn't think about that now. All that mattered was that he was getting better.

*She had a mate.* Wonder filled the corner of her heart before she forced herself to block it. Tiredness hit her and she realized how worried she'd been.

She listened to his even breathing and before she knew it, she fell asleep.

Airen stirred once more through the long night, and found herself wrapped in strong arms. She swore that she dreamed of lips at her temple.

The next thing she knew, she blinked open her eyes. Morning light streamed through the window.

There was a hot, hot body beside her.

She turned her head and found dark-gold eyes watching her.

She glanced down Donovan's chest. Her scales were gone from him and she swallowed. She wasn't going to tell him. She wouldn't force him to be with her, if that wasn't his choice.

Her gaze wandered over his skin. His *healed* skin. The wound was gone.

"How do you feel?" she asked.

"Alive," he said.

She smiled, then it faded with the remnants of worry. "It was close." Too close.

He yanked her down, his arms closing around her. She pressed her face to his chest, fighting back all the relieved emotions swelling inside her.

When Donovan released her, he rubbed a hand over his chest. "Our hosts must have some good meds."

She made a sound she hoped passed for agreement.

He sat up. "Damn, I feel great. No pain. Full range of movement." He shifted his shoulder. "I could eat a horse, but I have loads of energy."

She sat up as well. "You need some food?"

He nodded.

139

"Well, why don't you freshen up? There isn't much left to eat from what they left me, so I'll get you something from Sanya's people."

He grabbed her hand. "Thanks for being with me, Airen. Without you, I'd be dead."

She squeezed his fingers, pushing her raging emotions down. She rose from the bed.

"Airen?"

She turned, watching as he lounged on the furs.

"I like your outfit." He shot her a wide, white smile.

Fighting off a smile, she rolled her eyes and left the room.

# CHAPTER FOURTEEN

She was so happy that Donovan was okay.

Holding a small plate of food, Airen pushed open the door quietly. He might've gone back to sleep.

She froze.

He wasn't asleep.

He was still washing, standing naked beside the tub.

Heat slammed into her. She'd felt desire before, wanted sex before, but she'd never felt anything like this.

He was all hard muscle and sleek lines. She had a glorious, side-on view of his hard ass and thick, muscled thighs.

Airen let her gaze run over his back, and that beautiful, dark skin. Her hand shook with need and she crouched, setting the food down before she dropped it.

Sensing her, Donovan turned, his gaze meeting hers.

She closed the door behind her. His hand moved, the cloth running over his hard chest, leaving a trail of dampness. He moved lower to his delineated abs.

Her mouth went dry. She couldn't look away. He washed around his thick cock.

His thick, hardening cock.

"Come here, Airen." His voice was a deep rumble.

"You're hungry. I brought food." *By Alqin's axe,* her tongue felt thick.

"I'm hungry, but I don't want food right now." He held out a big, strong hand.

Those hands had held her up during this ordeal. They'd earned her trust.

She crossed the room, trembling. She'd never trembled before in her life.

He took her hand and pressed it to his chest. She felt his heart beating hard.

"What do you want, Airen?"

She blinked. Had anyone ever asked her that before? She'd fought hard to become a warrior, but no one had ever asked her what she wanted.

She brought her other hand up, marveling at her pale skin against the dark sheen of his. His strong body made her feel almost delicate, feminine. She went up on her toes and kissed him.

He growled against her lips, and kissed her back.

She slid her arms around his neck, her body pressed against all that naked maleness. His hard cock pressed against her belly.

She tore her mouth away. "I want you. Naked, on the bed, under me."

At her words, she felt his cock throb.

He smiled. "You giving me orders, Second Commander?"

She pushed him. "Yes."

This time, she was taking what she wanted.

He obeyed, dropping down, and stretching out on the bed.

Airen's mouth watered. *Oh, that body, that cock.* She moved to join him, but he held up a hand.

"Lose the trousers, Airen." He grinned. "But keep the top."

She felt humor shoot through her desire. She'd never smiled or felt the need to laugh during sex before. She unfastened the trousers and pushed them down her legs.

Donovan made a strangled sound and she straightened. His hot, gold gaze was on her.

She wasn't wearing any underwear. He stared at the tiny strip of hair at the juncture of her thighs, and she shifted, her thighs rubbing together. She was so wet.

Then she pressed one knee to the furs. She needed to touch him. Taste him. Staring down at that big muscled body, she felt like she was under a spell.

He stared up at her. "You have no idea how beautiful you are."

Her heart did a little tumble. She reached out and touched his abs, stroking the hard ridges. His hand came up and touched her breasts where they pushed up against the leather. They felt swollen, sensitive.

Airen straddled one of his thick thighs.

"Fuck, I can feel how wet you are," he bit out.

She stroked her hands over his chest, and scratched one intriguing nipple. He jerked. She lowered her head and licked the flat nub. He moaned.

His hand gripped her hip, bit in. Then his fingers whispered over her skin, moving between her legs.

She released a breathy moan. His fingers were between her thighs, stroking. She started to move against them.

"Yeah, that's it, sexy girl." He slid a thick finger inside her. Then another.

Airen bit her lip, trying to control her moans.

Donovan's big thumb rubbed her clitoris and she cried out.

"I see Eon women are similar to Terran women," he murmured.

"I need you." Her voice was thick.

"Good, because I'm all yours." He lay back, spread out for her.

She shifted, moving to circle his hard, swollen cock. She pumped it, liking the harsh sound that broke from his chest.

She lifted her hips and notched that cock between her legs.

Their gazes met, locked.

"Right now, you are the sexiest, hottest, most gorgeous thing I've ever seen," he growled.

With those words, Airen drove down on him.

"Christ." He groaned, his hips thrusting up.

She cried out, full of Donovan. That thick cock speared into her, stretching her to the point of pain.

"Move, Airen."

She did, rising and falling. She pressed her hands to his chest and started slow at first, building speed. It felt so good. She rocked, riding his cock, pleasure growing.

"Faster," he ordered, his hands on her hips. "You feel that?"

"Yes." She felt it all, too much, not enough.

Her climax was building, accompanied by a flutter of fear. It was so huge, intimidating.

Then he rose up to sitting with a flex of his muscles, until they were face-to-face. He kissed her, his tongue plunging against hers.

Airen came, filled with Donovan. She imploded, crying out his name, and her world flashed bright white.

A second later, he thrust into her, bit her bottom lip, groaning as he came. His cock throbbed inside her, his strong arms locked around her.

Holding her tight.

---

DONOVAN FELL BACK on the mattress, Airen's slim body on top of him.

He stroked her slick back. "You okay, baby?"

She nodded against his chest.

He slid his hand into the mass of her hair. Her sensible braid was deceptive. She had a lot of hair.

He smiled. He liked it spread over him. He cupped the back of her head, massaging gently.

"Thank you," she whispered.

His smile widened. She had absolutely no reason to thank him for what they'd just done together. "For what?"

She lifted her head, black-and-turquoise eyes meeting his. "For wanting me the way you do."

A dark weight pressed on his chest. Eon men were clearly idiots if they hadn't made this incredible woman feel cherished.

He urged her head up and kissed her deeply. When he pulled back, her face was a little dazed. He had planned for them to eat something, and then talk over their plan for getting off Oblivion. But then and there, he decided to have her again.

"We aren't leaving today," he said. They were safe enough hidden in this rocky fortress.

She nodded. "I think we both need a little more time to recover."

Donovan had no plans to spend the day napping. He was going to explore every inch of Airen, and make her come again. And again.

He rolled, spreading her out flat on the bed.

He watched her gaze sharpen. He undid the vest and pulled it off her.

Damn, she had pretty breasts. She was mouthwateringly gorgeous. He'd always dated fellow soldiers, once a firefighter, and a combat paramedic. He liked a warrior woman.

Airen was that, but she was also a hypnotic blend of hard and soft. Tough but sexy.

He lowered his head and sucked one nipple into his mouth. She moaned and he took his time. Once the nipple was hard, he moved to her other breast.

Glancing over, he spied the plate of food she'd brought for him. He rose and went to get it. When he turned, he found her hot gaze glued to his ass, then his cock.

He smiled. "Like what you see?"

Her gaze flicked up, color on her cheeks. "Yes."

He pressed a knee to the mattress and set the plate down. He spied a red berry and popped one into his mouth. *Mmm.* Tasted almost like a raspberry. He licked the red liquid off his fingers and saw Airen's breath hitch.

Grabbing another berry, he stretched out beside her. He pressed the small fruit to her lips, rubbing it over them. Then he painted across one pretty breast, streaking red on her pale skin. He circled her nipple with the berry and she gasped.

Lowering his head, Donovan followed the trail he'd made, lapping at her skin. He didn't know what tasted better, the tart berry or Airen's sweet skin. He took his time, sucking her nipple in his mouth. She arched into him.

"You're so sensitive," he murmured. Grabbing another berry, he painted lower.

Next, he pressed his mouth down her lightly muscled stomach. He pushed her thighs apart, painting red juice just above her mound. She made a husky, needy sound that he felt in his hard cock.

With the last of the berry, he touched her clit. The sound she made was guttural, her body as tight as a bow.

He popped the berry into his mouth, chewed, then swallowed. "Enjoy, Airen. I'm going to suck until you come."

Her chest hitched. "Donovan—"

He slid his tongue along her clit and her body rocked up. She pushed against his mouth.

Damn, the taste of her was better than any succulent

berry. He licked and sucked, clamping his hands on her hips and lifting her up to his hungry mouth.

*So damn good.* He could stay right here all day, eating her and wringing pleasure out of her. Soon, her cries were incoherent, and he heard a sob escape her. A second later, she came, her body shuddering, and his name—whispered hoarsely—the best thing he'd ever heard from her lips.

Donovan let her go and moved over her. His need was a raging thing. Something he'd never felt before welled inside him. A need to claim, to mark her as his.

She reached for him, but he was too on edge. He took both her wrists in one hand and pressed them to the bed above her head.

Eyes, threaded with brilliant green-turquoise, met his. His steel-hard cock was throbbing again, weeping.

"Now," she purred.

"I'm in charge this time," he growled.

He gripped his cock, positioned. Then he surged inside her.

They both groaned, her legs clamping around his hips. Damn, she was so slick, tight, and wet. He started moving, thrusting deep.

She met every thrust. "Donovan!" Need drenched her voice.

He kept his gaze on hers, driving hard, learning the feel of her where she was soft and silken.

"Faster," she urged.

"No. Slow." He swiveled his hips, thrusting in firmly, inexorably.

He wanted to make her feel what he was feeling. Right now, right here, they were one.

Donovan felt the pleasure building, coiling at the base of his spine. Damn, his next climax would take his head off. He started to move faster, his control slipping.

Her breathing was coming in pants.

"Don't come yet," he warned.

She moaned.

He slid a hand between their thrusting bodies and found her swollen clit.

"*Donovan.*" Her body jerked.

"Not yet, baby."

She arched up, making a mewling, desperate cry.

He thrust hard. Jesus, so warm, so tight. He thumbed her clit again. "Now, Airen."

Her back arched, her head thrust back against the furs. As she cried out, her body clamped on his.

Donovan pounded into her through her climax, then his own release hit him like a blow.

He lowered his head and sank his teeth into the vulnerable point where her neck met her shoulder. She cried out again and he spilled inside her, groaning her name, his world reduced to nothing but Airen.

---

AIREN OPENED her mouth and Donovan slid a slice of fruit between her lips.

They were both lying on the bed, him propped up on one elbow, gloriously naked, as he fed her.

She wasn't sure she'd ever felt this relaxed, or well-used. Her muscles were loose and languid. They'd spent the entire day making love. At times it had been playful, other times intense. Donovan was a generous lover.

Her gaze slid over his strong body—the heavy muscles, the thick cock resting against his thigh. She loved looking at him.

He reached out, fiddling with her hair. "How you doing, sexy girl?"

She smiled. "Good. How's your injury?"

He rubbed his still-healing shoulder. "Feels better and better."

A knock at the door made them both sit up. Donovan rose, grabbed a drying cloth from beside the tub, and wrapped it around his waist. Airen pulled a woven blanket up over her naked body.

He opened the door to show a leather-clad warrior in the doorway. The woman ran an appreciative gaze down Donovan's body before she straightened. "Sanya requests your company for the evening meal."

"Great," he replied. "Tell her we'll be there." He closed the door and Airen stood. His gaze ran over her naked body, heating. "Hmm, you'd better wear something other than that."

She tossed him a look, pulling on her leather trousers and vest. She worked on re-braiding her hair.

Donovan's spacesuit was damaged, so he sawed the damaged top half off with a knife, just leaving the bottom half as his trousers. He pulled a leather vest out of the clothes that had been left for them, and slipped it on.

Her pulse jumped. He looked like a dangerous

marauder. Moving closer, she touched his healing wound. It looked much better.

His long fingers circled her wrist. "It's healing well. I feel great." He nipped her lips. "Although, having my cock deep inside you most of the day might have something to do with that."

"Inappropriate," she murmured.

"Totally." He bit her bottom lip. "Let's go see our host."

When they entered the large great room, most of the residents were eating at low tables while sitting on pillows. Most conversation stopped and people stared. Airen hated the wary, distrusting, and sometimes scared looks cast Donovan's way. She wasn't worried about him, just hated knowing that these women had suffered.

Sanya was seated alone at a table at the front of the room. Through the windows behind her, Airen saw the darkening night sky.

The leader rose, her gaze meeting Donovan's. "It's good to see you on your feet, warrior."

"Happy to be back on my feet. And it's Donovan."

Sanya nodded, then with a small smile, looked at Airen. "You both look...refreshed."

Airen felt her cheeks heat. "Thank you again. For everything."

Sanya waved a hand at the table. "Please sit. Eat."

The plates on the table were loaded with simple, but interesting-looking foods. Airen and Donovan settled on the pillows.

"Crux and his monsters are still lurking near the hot

pools." Sanya said. "We also saw a Kantos swarm ship flying nearby."

Airen sucked in a breath. "We need to leave, Sanya. I won't bring the Kantos down on you."

"We can deal with a few little bugs."

"They have a lot of dangerous creatures." Airen looked around the room, at the children. "You can't risk it."

"And we need to get off this planet and find our people," Donovan added.

"No one gets off Oblivion," Sanya said.

He crossed his arms over his chest. "We will."

"We need to get to the prison command," Airen said.

Sanya's gaze was steady. "You're going to try and get through the planetary net."

Airen nodded.

The leader's lips pressed together. "The prison command is two islands away from here, but for tonight, you can't go anywhere. And I don't think either of you are at full strength." She picked up a bread roll. "Please, enjoy our hospitality. My scouts are watching for the Kantos. For now, you can relax."

Trying to traverse Oblivion's terrain in the dark would be a foolish risk. Airen lifted a fork and speared some flaky, cooked fish.

Sanya lifted a glass of ruby-red drink. "Airen tells me we share another enemy, Donovan." Her face hardened as she sipped her drink. "The Kantos."

"Fuckers," Donovan bit out.

"They destroyed my planet. I hope you can save

yours, Donovan." She set her glass down and picked up a fork. "Now, enough talk of bugs."

The meal was good, and the wine was light, delicious, and fizzed pleasantly in Airen's belly.

"You make this wine?" she asked.

Sanya's smile was full of pride. "We do. Our sanctuary is completely self-sufficient. We fish, farm, have an orchard, mill, brew, make our wine." She lifted her glass. "Everyone here shares their unique skills and talents."

"Your healers are amazing," Donovan said. "My wound is almost healed. On Earth, even with our tech, we can't match that."

Sanya's gaze met Airen's. Airen shook her head, hoping the leader would help keep her secret.

Thankfully, Sanya changed the subject, talking about her warriors and their training sessions. Donovan leaned forward, joining the discussion.

Airen watched him, feeling relaxed and happy. He drank some wine and she watched the strong column of his throat as he swallowed. A flash of heat bloomed in her belly. *Cren*, watching the man drink aroused her. Somehow this Terran man had turned her into a sex-obsessed woman.

He shifted, his thigh pressing against hers under the table. At first, she thought it was accidental, as his focus was still on Sanya. But then his hand moved onto her thigh, his clever fingers stroking up her leg. As hunger ignited, she quickly sipped her drink.

"We plan to leave tomorrow," Donovan said.

Airen fought to focus. "We can't risk bringing the Kantos down on you, and we need to get off this planet."

Sanya sat back. "It's a dangerous journey to the prison command, but I understand."

"We have to get back to our ship and people," Airen said, covering Donovan's hand with hers.

"We should get some sleep," he said. "Thanks again, Sanya, the meal was delicious."

The leader bowed her head. "Sleep well."

Rising, Donovan tugged Airen to her feet. They headed out of the great room and into the corridor leading to their room.

He jerked her to a halt and spun her into him. His mouth took hers, hungry and demanding. "I need you."

"Yes," she moaned.

They hurried to their room, and once inside, she noted someone had cleaned and left an oil lamp lit. Donovan slammed her back against the wall, his mouth claiming hers. She felt a desperate need and was so hungry for him that she was shocked by the torrent of emotion inside her.

She tore at his vest and he helped her get it off. Then she spun them so he was pressed against the wall. Her hands attacked his trousers.

"Airen—"

"I want to taste you." She shoved the fabric down, freeing his thick cock. With a humming sound, she dropped to her knees.

He made a deep growl and she pressed her hands to his muscular thighs. She grasped his cock with one hand, then lowered her mouth to the swollen head.

He groaned, and she licked, savoring the salty taste of him. Taking her time, she worked his thickness into her mouth. He sank one hand into her hair, thrusting into her mouth.

"Jesus..." Suddenly, he pulled her off him and yanked her up. His hands jerked off her trousers. "No more. I need to fuck you. *Now*."

He lifted her up and pinned her to the wall, his big hands palming her ass. She hooked her legs around his waist, undulating against him. He moved one hand between them, taking his cock in hand, then he pushed inside her.

"*Donovan*." She gasped and arched into him. She'd been so empty, but now, she was so wonderfully full.

He thrust deep. "Hold tight, sexy girl. It's going to be a hard, rough ride."

His mouth was on hers again, the kiss scorching hot. She rocked against him.

"Don't let go," she panted.

He ground against her. "Never."

# CHAPTER FIFTEEN

A iren sat at the small window, on a small, carved-stone bench, watching Oblivion's sun rise. She had a gorgeous view of the island and ocean below, and it looked beautiful. It was easy to forget that this was a prison planet with dangers lurking.

After the day and night she'd spent with Donovan, she'd completely forgotten where she was. There had only been Donovan and pleasure. So much pleasure.

Her mate.

He slept behind her on the bed, but she didn't let herself look at him. Her nails bit into her palms.

She could never tell him that they were mated. Her helian became agitated. It wanted to link with him, bathe in the joy.

She didn't hear him move—for a big man, he moved very quietly—but she felt him press in behind her. His heat engulfed her, his now familiar masculine scent filled her.

"Good morning." He pressed a kiss to her bare shoulder. She was only wrapped loosely in a fur.

"Good morning." She tilted her head to give him better access. His lips felt so good.

"What's wrong, baby? I sense you're lost in your thoughts."

She looked blindly out the window. "We have to go." She needed to focus on the most pressing problem first. "The longer we stay, the greater the risk the Kantos will find us. We're putting these people at risk."

Donovan rubbed his jaw on her shoulder. "Reality is intruding."

In so many kinds of ways. She felt a desperate clutch in her belly.

Then she turned and kissed him. She needed him. Just one more time—she wanted the weight of him on her, the smell of him on her skin.

He groaned against her lips, his hands sliding and clenching in her hair. He liked burying his hands in her hair.

"I need you," she whispered.

"Anything, baby."

The kiss deepened, taking on a hungry edge.

Then Donovan dropped to his knees in front of her, pushed the fur away and her legs apart.

"So damn beautiful, especially here." He stroked between her folds.

Sensations rocketed through her. It was so easy to lose herself in this man.

He lowered his head, and then his mouth was on her.

"Donovan." *Oh, by the warriors.*

She pressed her hands to his head, feeling his short hair, and she let her own head drop back. He kept licking and sucking. Airen could no more hold back her orgasm, than she could a tidal wave.

She came, her body shaking, his name on her lips.

Before she'd recovered, he turned her and she found her hips pressed to the bench. His big body pressed against her from behind, and anticipation was like a sharp blade against her skin.

She felt the nudge of his cock, then he slid inside her.

"There it is." He started thrusting, his mouth at her ear. "Feels so damn good to be inside you. Like sliding home."

Soon, there was no talking. She thrust back against him, and his hands moved beneath her body. His clever fingers found her clit.

Airen exploded again, the pleasure so acute. She cried out his name. After another deep thrust, Donovan followed her. He groaned as his big body shuddered.

After they caught their breath, they rose, and he pulled her into his arms. "Whatever happens outside this room, we're together. We've got this."

She nodded, wanting to believe that was true. She was a warrior, and she was well aware of the risks they'd face as soon as they stepped out of this room.

They cleaned up and Airen once again commanded her helian to form her armor. Donovan pulled on his spacesuit trousers and vest.

He caught her gaze and nodded. They headed out of the room, making their way to the great room. Women and children sat around eating, but today she did note a few old men and a couple of teenaged boys.

Sanya and Tira met them.

"Thank you again, Sanya," Airen said. "We wouldn't have survived without your help."

The warrior leader nodded. "We wish you both the best of luck getting to the prison command."

Tira eyed them. "The prison command island is to the west, two islands from here."

"Great." Donovan nodded. "So we'll need a boat."

"It's not that easy," the warrior added. "The ocean here is deadly."

"We know the risks," Airen said.

Sanya shook her head. "The wardens generate wild, rogue waves. They take out anything stupid enough to be on the water."

Airen's stomach tightened.

"And the water is filled with genetically engineered bots and animals designed to stop prisoners from moving around. They tear people to shreds."

*Cren.* Airen met Donovan's gaze.

He lifted his chin. "We have to try."

———

STANDING ON THE BEACH, Donovan surveyed the water.

A few children played on the sand behind him, under the watchful eye of some women. Sanya's warriors had brought out a wooden raft.

*Shit.* It wasn't much.

159

The leader shrugged. "We don't go out on the water. Ever. This washed up one day, no doubt from someone foolish enough to try and cross between islands."

Donovan glanced at the water again. It looked calm today, like glass.

"The prison command is on the island beyond that one." Sanya pointed.

Beside them, Airen stood staring, her hands on her hips.

Damn, he loved her in her armor. He needed to get his unruly cock under control. Usually, after he'd spent a long, sweaty night or two with a woman, it took the edge off his desire. Apparently with Airen, it just made it worse.

He forced himself to look at the islands. The one ahead of them was a long line of sharp mountains.

"Here." A woman with dark-blonde hair and ragged skirts appeared. She didn't look at him, but she nodded at Airen and handed over a small leather pack. "Food. Water. Some medicines."

"Thank you," Airen said quietly. She looked back at Sanya. "I will let the Eon High Command know that you helped us. We could get you off this planet."

The leader gave her a small smile. "For better or worse, this is our home. Most of us have no homeworld to go to, or if we do, we aren't welcome there, anyway."

With a nod, Airen clasped hands with the woman in a warrior's grasp.

Donovan nodded at the leader. Then he and Airen grabbed the raft and pushed it down the sand toward the water.

Just then, shouts and screams broke out behind them.

They swiveled, and Donovan saw several Kantos race out onto the sand.

"*Cren!*" Airen dropped the raft and took off running. Tira was one step behind her, drawing a sword.

Sanya yelled at her people. "Get everyone inside!"

Women ran, snatching up children.

Even while running, Airen managed to create a blaster. She shot a bolt of green energy at the Kantos.

"Weapon," Donovan barked.

Sanya waved to one of her warriors. A muscular woman stepped forward and handed him a sword.

His hand closed on the hilt. It was much better crafted than Crux's crappy, makeshift weapons.

Donovan ran. Warriors assembled around him, pulling out staffs, crossbows, and swords.

Ahead, Tira was fighting a Kantos soldier. Airen had her sword formed now, and was a deadly blur as she broke through a group of the aliens.

With a roar, Donovan attacked the closest Kantos.

The alien soldier spun, its beady eyes glowing. Two female warriors threw a net and it tangled around the Kantos' body. As it tripped onto the sand, Donovan leaped on top of it and drove his sword down.

All around him, the female warriors fought viciously to protect their people and their home.

Soon, the sand was covered in green blood and dead Kantos.

Donovan moved over to Airen. He gave her body a long look and didn't see any injuries. She nodded.

Then suddenly, a long, lean woman ran out of the

trees at a sprint. She wore a tiny leather skirt and sleeveless top.

"One of our scouts," Sanya said.

"More aliens are coming," the scout yelled.

Airen's jaw went tight.

"Go," Sanya said to them. "We can fight the Kantos off."

Damn, Donovan didn't want to leave them with this. Airen looked conflicted too.

He pressed a hand to her shoulder. "If we go, there's a chance the Kantos will lose interest in our friends here."

Airen nodded slowly. "Thank you again, Sanya."

"Be well, Airen Kann-Felis. Good luck to you and your man."

Donovan held out the sword to the warrior who'd given it to him.

The woman shook her head. "Keep it. I suspect you'll need it."

He took the scabbard another warrior offered him, and strapped it onto his back. He reached over his shoulder and slid the sword into place.

He and Airen moved back to the raft, and pushed it out into the water. It was no longer like glass, but the waves were fairly gentle. He grabbed the oars and handed her one.

They pushed the raft up past the breaking waves, and then climbed onto the raft and started paddling.

Soon, they were working together, and picking up speed.

He glanced back at the beach and saw Sanya's warriors fighting the Kantos.

"We need to skirt that first island and get into the open water," Airen said.

He nodded, and when he looked down to where his paddle was cutting into the water, a large shadow moved beneath the raft.

A big one.

Primal fear spilled down his spine. There was a reason he preferred space to water. *Fuck. Just keep paddling, Lennox.*

The wind picked up, and soon they were moving around the first island. Airen was tense, but focused.

The swells grew larger, taking them up and then dropping them down in between each wave. They got closer to the island, and he stared at the black rock hills. They were dotted with some black, leafless trees. Lava dripped down in places to sizzle as it met the ocean.

"Almost clear of the first island." She shot him a smile.

He smiled back.

They rounded the tip of the island, and ahead lay open ocean.

The shadow of a second island lay in the distance, and there was the silhouette of a large tower in the center.

The prison command base.

"There it is," Airen said.

"We've got this, Second Commander."

That earned him a small smile.

They kept paddling.

"I keep waiting for something to happen." He felt like he was walking on damn eggshells.

"I feel the same." She frowned. "Wait. Where did the island go?"

His head whipped up. He could no longer see the prison command tower. He frowned. It had just been there, now he could only see water.

They kept paddling, dread building.

Then he blinked. "Oh, fuck."

"What?" She peered at the horizon, then stiffened.

A huge wall of water was building in front of them, blocking the view of the island.

An enormous, rogue wave, kilometers wide.

They both stopped paddling and watched as the wave started to loom high above them. It was the largest wave Donovan had ever seen.

"Donovan—"

"We have to ride it out. Hold on!"

Their raft started climbing the wave, getting steeper and steeper.

They both pressed flat against the wood, and suddenly, he saw a black rope snake out from Airen's armor, tying them both onto the raft.

He grabbed her hand, entwined their fingers. Then his stomach dropped. They were near the crest of the wave, the steepness threatening to drop them back down into the water.

*Fuck.*

They crested the top and then dropped, tipping over the other side of the giant wall of water. Water crashed down over them, flipping them over.

Donovan tried to yell Airen's name, but his mouth filled with water.

Then everything was just bubbles, water, and tumbling over and over.

# CHAPTER SIXTEEN

Cren. *Cren.*

Airen tumbled over and over, with no idea which way was up. Without thought, her helian formed a helmet over her head and she could breathe again.

*Donovan.* She reached out and felt hard flesh. But he didn't have the ability to morph a helmet. *Please be okay.* They were both still lashed to the raft, and spinning out of control.

Then suddenly, they slammed downward with a huge splash of water. The crazy tumbling stopped, and they bobbed up and down.

Airen quickly retracted her helmet and the ropes.

"Donovan." He lay limply beside her on the raft. "Donovan!"

He lifted his head and spat out some water. "Ugh."

Relief flooded her. She grabbed his face and kissed him. They were both saturated, her hair was plastered to her head.

She looked over her shoulder and saw that the rogue

wave was gone, absorbed back into the ocean like it had never been there.

"You're sure you're okay?" She patted his arms.

"I am now. Hell of a ride."

They both sat up and looked ahead. The prison command tower was clearer now.

The island was ringed by a wide, sandy beach, and in the center were metal walls, spearing up into the sky, protecting the warden base. Several smaller scout towers dotted the wall. She could see now that the central tower had a landing pad on top. A ship was parked on it.

"Look, Donovan."

He eyed the ship and nodded. "Our ticket out of here."

But they still had a long way to go to get there.

"Shit," he muttered. "Look at the beach."

Several large, metal boxes, about the size of a land transport, were spaced out around the beach. She frowned.

"They're turrets," he said. "Some sort of cannons, I'm guessing."

She sucked in a breath. They'd have to run the gauntlet to get through them and reach the main building.

Donovan bumped his shoulder against hers. "You like a challenge, right?"

She huffed out a breath. "Right."

The oars were long gone, so they both lay flat, with their legs over the edge, and started kicking.

They were making slow but steady progress, when light glinted off something in the water ahead of them.

"Did you see that?" she asked.

Donovan's dark gaze narrowed. "Yeah, I see it."

"Can you tell what it is?"

"No, but the way our day's going, it's not going to be good."

Even with her enhanced vision, Airen couldn't quite make out what was floating on the water. She could tell there were several small objects. "Maybe it's just fish?"

He snorted skeptically.

They got closer, and she saw that the objects were metallic, disc-shaped, and about the size of her hand. Then they started spinning through the water, splashing at the surface.

*Uh-oh*. Her muscles tensed.

She saw the objects start toward them. They were covered in sharp spikes that speared out of the water. They formed a deadly line.

"Look out!" she yelled.

They both leaped off the raft. The spikes ran through the center of it, slicing it in two.

Donovan came up, treading water and Airen did the same. They spun, watching as the bots circled around them like a pack of deadly animals.

Airen commanded her helian to form a weapon.

"Fuck, they're coming at us," Donovan yelled.

The spikes closed in. Airen's helian let out a pulse of energy that made a dull boom.

The spikes stopped, bobbing in the water like their batteries had run dry.

"Electromagnetic pulse," she said. "They're disabled."

He released a long breath. "Have I told you that you are amazing?"

She smiled. He made her feel amazing.

They righted part of the raft, and she frowned. "Our ride is a little less spacious now."

"I don't mind. I like being close to you." He winked.

Airen couldn't help but smile again. They climbed on and started kicking. They hadn't gone far when he tensed.

"What now?" she demanded.

"There's something swimming under us. Keep kicking."

All of a sudden, a long, thin tentacle rose up out of the water nearby.

*By Ston's sword.* A shiver skated down Airen's spine.

The tentacle whipped out and slapped into Donovan. It knocked him into the water, and he spluttered.

Airen peered into the dark water, trying to see what this creature was.

Suddenly, Donovan was yanked under the surface.

"No!" She dived under the water and saw the creature now. It had a large, bullet-shaped body, huge eyes, and lots of wildly waving tentacles.

It was covered in deep, dark-green scales. She couldn't see any metal, so it wasn't a bot. Maybe it wasn't as dangerous?

Great, she was grading monsters now. She grabbed Donovan's hand and yanked. Strangely, the creature released him, and they both broke the surface.

A moment later, the creature did too, its pointed head bobbing above the water.

"I'm cancelling that beach holiday I had booked," Donovan muttered.

The creature looked at them with its giant eyes. Then it used a tentacle to splash them with water. The movement was almost...playful.

"Ah, hi," Airen said.

Donovan's head swiveled. "You're going to talk to it?"

"I think it's trying to be friendly." A tentacle moved tentatively toward her. She stayed still, and it reached up and touched her hair. "It's curious."

The tentacle moved over her face. Something poked out the end of it and ran down her cheek. It felt slimy.

Donovan raised a brow. "I think it's licking you."

She gently pushed the tentacle away. "We don't have time to play. We need to go there." She pointed to the island.

The creature sank back into the water with a ripple. *Oh.* "Bye."

Donovan looked at the island. "Airen, they'll have lookouts, security surveillance. By the time we swim up to them, they'll have seen us coming. They'll no doubt turn the gun turrets on us."

She dragged in a breath, trying to think of a better plan. "I guess—"

Two tentacles broke out of the water and wrapped around their waists.

Airen gasped and gripped the scaly appendage.

"Damn, I think your friend got hungry," Donovan said.

She tried to pry the tentacle off her.

Then they both jerked as the tentacles moved. Their

friend appeared out of the water, then took off toward the island, moving fast.

Airen cried out. She and Donovan were being towed behind the creature at lightning speed.

---

THE PRISON COMMAND island drew nearer at a breakneck pace. Water splashed Donovan's face and he turned his head to the side, struggling not to swallow too much of it.

A second later, he and Airen were tossed up on the sand.

"*Oof.*" Airen spun on her hands and knees.

Donovan coughed up some water. A tentacle flicked out of the water and gave Airen's cheek another lick. Then the creature disappeared back beneath the surface.

"I'm dizzy." She moved into a crouch, wringing water out of her braid.

Donovan shook his head in disbelief, then focused on the gun emplacement nearby. "Come on, we're too exposed here."

The creature's actions were a stroke of luck, and he wasn't going to waste it. They ran together, ducking down beside the metallic box of the turret to avoid detection.

"Do you think they have thermal scanners?" she asked.

"Not sure." He would have them, if he were in charge of this place, but maybe the wardens believed that the ocean and the creatures in it were enough of a deterrent to the planet's residents.

He studied the main walls of the base ahead. Heavy-duty metal and very high. Large doors were set into the wall, but with no obvious way to open them. It looked like a futuristic castle.

"You think we can get those doors open?" he asked.

She considered. "I might be able to hack into the control system. We need to get there first."

They both looked at the row of turret emplacements.

Then she smiled. "Ready for a little run, Sub-Captain?"

"I'll fight by your side any day, Second Commander."

There was a flash in her eyes, a warmth that softened his warrior's face. Donovan grabbed her and pressed a quick kiss to her lips.

Then they both rose and started jogging toward the wardens' base.

There was a snick of sound. Donovan turned. Another snick and he saw metal panels moving on the turret box. His blood ran cold.

A turret rose up out of the center and swiveled in their direction.

"Run!"

They sprinted across the sand. Laser fire broke out and they both dived, rolling across the ground.

The laser cut into the sand. It was so powerful, it changed the sand, leaving hunks of glass behind.

They both leaped up, and another turret emplacement ahead opened.

Donovan grabbed Airen and threw her into the air. She dived over the top of the turret.

Laser fire tore up the sand near him and he dodged. He ran as fast as he could, but the laser arced closer.

He pumped his arms and legs. Air sawed in and out of his lungs.

Suddenly, Airen leaped onto the top of the turret and lifted her arm. She rammed a black-scaled spear down into the turret, and the blast cut off.

Donovan slid in beside the turret box and she leaped down.

"Are you all right?" she asked.

He nodded and they swiveled to look at the building. Several wardens were visible now—all wearing dark uniforms and helmets—standing on top of the walls of the base.

"Okay, what's our next move?" he asked.

There was a rush of sound and they both looked up. Donovan expected to see some sort of ship belonging to the wardens.

Instead, several Kantos swarm ships filled the sky.

"Oh, fuck."

Bugs swarmed out of the side of the ships, dropping down toward the beach. He spotted several Kantos soldiers arrowing down as well.

One swarm landed to the north side of the beach, and the other to the south.

Airen and Donovan were trapped in the middle of them.

"*Cren.*" Her face looked grim.

All around them, bugs hit the sand. There were so

many different types. Some were smaller, about the size of a dog. Many were larger, towering over Donovan. A number of the creatures had huge horns on the front of them, and brown, hard-shelled bodies.

"We need to get to the wardens," Airen said. "Maybe they'll let us in."

He snorted. "Yeah, right."

"Then we'll let ourselves in," she said.

They broke into a run.

All around them, the turrets opened across the beach. The weapons swiveled, firing on the Kantos bugs. But there were so many of them, wave after wave. Donovan saw one large bug with a huge, bulging body stop and open its huge mouth. It proceeded to vomit out smaller bugs.

Laser fire cut close to Donovan and Airen. They both dived and rolled. They came up, facing a large bug. Donovan pulled out his sword and, with a vicious swing, sliced the bug's head off. Green blood splattered his chest.

Airen had morphed her weapon into a sword and was cutting through several others.

"Keep moving!" she yelled.

Ahead, he saw the doors of the warden base opening.

Rows of armed wardens marched out, rifles clutched in their hands.

Suddenly, a large bug landed in front of Donovan and Airen, making the ground shake.

It had two sturdy legs and four arms, a bulky body covered in a light layer of fur, and pincers on its mouth. It pounded its muscular chest, reminding Donovan of a gorilla. It was almost as though a gorilla and a bug had mated. He grimaced at the idea.

Airen didn't pause. She rushed at the alien, attacking hard. She ducked a swing of one of its arms, but before her sword made contact, one of its other three arms grabbed her. It lifted her off her feet and threw her through the air.

*No.* Donovan charged. The gorilla-bug spun, hammering its fists into the ground. Donovan jumped up, but midair, the creature hit him like a speeding starship.

Pain crashed into him. Damn, the thing was strong.

Donovan hit the ground hard, sliding through the sand. He shook his head. *Shit.*

He blinked his eyes and saw Airen leap up. She kicked the creature in the head and it roared. As she dropped, she swung her sword fast, and sliced open the gorilla-bug's gut.

*That's my girl.*

Screams filled the air, and Donovan whipped his head around. The bugs were swarming the wardens.

As he watched, one bug rammed its horn into a warden's head, right through the soldier's helmet. It lifted the warden's body off the ground, and the warden jerked wildly.

*What the fuck?*

"We need to get inside," Airen said urgently.

He turned, and saw more bugs stabbing the wardens' heads.

Airen grimaced. "Donovan. Now."

"What are they doing?"

"Sucking out their brain matter."

Donovan winced. *Great.*

He ran with Airen, and they tried to circle the attacking bugs. But every way they moved, more bugs rushed at them.

They were still too far away from the building. A second later, they were surrounded.

He took a step forward, but several bugs darted closer, lots of them with those deadly, brain-sucking horns.

"Donovan." Airen looked around warily.

Yeah, there was no way out.

All of a sudden, an injured, blood-covered warden ran at them wildly. The bugs scattered, swiveling to face the incoming man.

Donovan seized the opportunity and grabbed Airen's hand. "Let's go."

Then he felt her body jerk.

He looked back, and saw her face was pale, her mouth open. His gaze dropped and his mind went blank.

There was a horn protruding through her stomach.

Her mouth moved, blood dripping from her lips.

Pain stormed through him. "Airen!"

# CHAPTER SEVENTEEN

Agony had a flavor. It was harsh, bitter, and overpowering.

Airen stared at the horn protruding from her body, tasted the blood in her mouth. Black ooze dripped from the horn, crawling up her chest.

*How had it pierced her armor?* Then she realized her helian was writhing. This black ooze was destabilizing her helian's abilities.

Her gaze locked with Donovan's. His face was twisted in horror, pain.

He touched his own stomach, like he felt her wound.

*Oh no.* She felt her helian pulsing, and knew that he was sharing what she felt.

He ran at her.

Airen summoned the last of her strength. She pulled herself off the bug's horn and turned, swinging her sword.

The alien bug dropped, buzzing as it died. The black ooze was crawling all over her now, multiplying.

"Airen?"

Donovan reached her just as she dropped to her knees.

"Donovan." A scratchy whisper.

"It's okay. You'll be okay." His hands were touching her.

It was a lie. They both knew it.

"Get off this planet." She clutched his hand. "Promise me...you'll make the Kantos pay."

He muttered a curse. "We'll do it together, Airen."

She cupped his face. She'd gotten so used to these strong lines. The thought of never seeing them again... The pain made her gasp.

"What the hell?" He was staring at the black ooze running over her. It was moving down her arm.

Her helian started to scream inside her, and she gasped.

"Airen?" He shook her a little.

"It's...targeting my helian."

The ooze was trying to separate her helian from her. It was ripping at the bonds between them.

Blindly, she stared at the fighting wardens and bugs. She could also see Kantos soldiers running in their direction.

"Donovan, go."

"Hell the fuck no." He plunged a hand into the ooze, tearing it off her. It was sticky and clung to his fingers. He threw it on the ground, but on her body, it kept multiplying and moving upward, covering her chest and neck.

One of the Kantos soldiers broke through the fighting. Donovan leaped up, swinging his sword. She watched him fight hard, so brutal and brave.

Her man. Her mate.

Agony hit her in another wave and she tried to scream. Her mouth was covered with the black ooze, and she coughed and choked.

She saw him slice at the Kantos soldier, then he raced back to her side. He dropped down and scooped her up in his arms.

He charged through the fighting, carrying her, using a booted foot to kick a bug out of his way. She fought to open her mouth, but the ooze covered it. She couldn't talk. Panic rose inside of her.

"Airen, what's happening?" He scraped the ooze away from her mouth, and she took a deep, shuddering breath.

"It's...trying to break the bond with my helian." The words came out garbled.

Searing, burning pain gripped her, her helian screaming in her head. She thought she heard splashing sounds.

Then suddenly, Donovan was dunking her in the water. "Fuck. *Fuck.*" He was trying to wash the ooze off her.

Several bugs ran at them, and Donovan tensed.

Then there was a froth of bubbles near them. Tentacles flew out of the waves, stabbing at the incoming aliens.

"Your friend's back, Airen." He pulled her close, still scrubbing the black ooze away.

The pain started to ease. She drew in a harsh breath.

Their tentacled friend stabbed at several bugs until the Kantos hung back, not daring to attack.

Donovan touched the helian band around her wrist. It was free of the ooze now.

"The pain has...lessened." The tearing feeling had gone, replaced with the regular aches and pains of her injuries. She dragged in a deep breath.

Donovan had saved her.

He smiled, and her helian pulsed.

Full awareness clicked back into place, and she heard the turrets firing, the wardens attacking, the ear-piercing screech of some of the Kantos bugs.

Their aquatic friend was still guarding them, attacking any bugs that dared get too close.

Suddenly, a Kantos soldier broke through with a huge jump. It landed on its four legs, beady eyes locked on them.

Donovan leaped up. He swung his sword at the alien, connecting with its sharp arm. They traded several hard blows, and then she heard a snapping sound.

Donovan's sword had broken in half.

Sensing weakness, the Kantos swiveled and skewered Donovan through his thigh with its arm. Donovan roared, going down on one knee.

His blood washed into the water around them.

The red made Airen's heart pound. She drew on what strength she had left. She was so weak, but she wouldn't let this Kantos hurt Donovan.

Her black scales flowed over her and then flowed across the air, hitting Donovan. They spread over his body.

He jolted, his eyes widening. Then she felt his emotions inside her—his shock, disbelief, relief. She also felt her helian working to heal his wounds, as her black-scale armor covered him.

A second later, Donovan rose, an Eon sword forming on his arm. He glared at the Kantos, which skittered backward several steps.

With a roar, Donovan attacked.

---

FEAR AND FURY were a potent mix.

Add in a rush of power from Airen's helian, and Donovan felt fucking ready to kill every risk to Airen on the beach. He felt the wound on his thigh closing up and healing.

He lifted his new, amazing sword, then glanced down at himself. He was covered in black-scale armor that matched Airen's. He knew what this meant, but now wasn't the time to think about it.

He charged at the Kantos. *The enemy.*

His sword hit the Kantos' arm. They traded blows, kicking up sand across the beach.

Donovan swiveled, shifting his weight, and sliced one of the Kantos' arms off. Green blood sprayed, and the Kantos jerked. Donovan leaped into the air, sword swinging.

They'd hurt Airen. They'd pay.

He spun and sliced the Kantos' head off.

Then he turned.

Airen was still on her knees, the waves lapping at her. She had a hand pressed to the horrible wound on her stomach, and blood rocked gently in the water around her.

His stomach felt like a rock. She was badly hurt, and while her helian would be helping her, he knew that helians couldn't fix every wound. They couldn't bring people back from death.

A bunch of bugs and wardens fought nearby. Donovan ducked past them, running to Airen. He dropped down beside her.

"Hey." He touched her face.

"Hey." Her voice was so soft and weak.

"Hanging in there?"

Her face was bone white, lines around her eyes. She managed a nod.

"So, we're mated, huh?"

She licked her lips, her face unreadable.

He cocked his head. "You knew?"

A small nod.

And she hadn't been planning to tell him. Anger burned through his gut. Not at his mate, but at everything and everyone in her life that had made the armored walls around her so thick.

He kissed her. Hard. Demanding.

Then he let loose what had been growing inside him for days, scaring the hell out of him so much. "I love you, Airen."

Her eyes widened in fear, wonder, and shock. "You said you didn't believe in love. That it was toxic and not real and—"

"I was an idiot who didn't know what he was talking

about. A frightened idiot who just needed a brave, beautiful warrior to show him the way."

She lifted a hand, but at that moment he heard engines. They both turned their heads and saw the spaceship on the prison command tower firing up its engines.

*Shit.*

"How about we get off this rock?" he said.

He helped her up, heard her groan. He hated seeing her in pain.

*The female is mine.*

The elite's voice cut through Donovan's head. Gritting his teeth, he lifted Airen into his arms.

"No, fucker, she's mine."

Resolute, he headed toward the prison command building. He sliced into an attacking bug, but kept striding forward.

Then he spotted the elite with two soldiers flanking him.

"Put me down," she said.

His hands tightened on her.

"I want to fight," she said. "I'm a warrior."

She was too hurt. "Airen—"

Her gaze met his, firm and unyielding. "I'm going to fight." She drew in a breath. "I don't know anything about love, Donovan, but what I feel for you...I don't have words to describe it."

He smiled. He'd take it. He and his warrior could learn all about love together. Every day for the rest of their lives.

If they got out of here alive.

She was shaky on her feet, but she formed her sword.

They attacked together.

Donovan sliced and diced into the bugs. The elite was hiding behind the soldiers. Donovan tackled one soldier, knocking the Kantos over.

Airen was there, slashing with her sword. She was in pain, but she was still a formidable fighter. She left her soldier dead and advanced on the elite.

*You can't stop us. You might win some battles, but you won't win this war.*

"Fuck you," Donovan said. "You'll never understand how to work with others. You consume, destroy, risk all your bugs like they're nothing." He looked at Airen. "The Eon and Earth are forming unbreakable bonds. You can *never* destroy those. We'll find other allies, we'll work together, and we'll stop your invasions and destruction."

Another rush of sound. More Kantos ships appeared in the sky, disgorging more bugs.

*Fuck.* Donovan glared at the elite.

*Pretty words, but they mean nothing against the never-ending might of the Kantos.*

The elite attacked. Donovan dodged, his blade striking the Kantos' chest, and leaving a deep groove in the hard shell.

Airen rushed in from the other side. She slammed her sword into the alien's leg, but with its arm, the elite shoved her back.

With a growl, Donovan charged, swinging wildly.

The Kantos whirled and slammed into Donovan, knocking him to his knees.

The elite lifted its arm, ready for an executioner's swing at Donovan's head.

"No!" Airen was struggling to get to her feet, holding her injured abdomen.

Suddenly, wild, undulating war cries filled the air.

The elite froze. An arrow slammed into the elite's head, right through its eye.

All over the beach, bugs swiveled. Donovan spun and saw Sanya, Tira, and dozens of female warriors sailing in on the waves, riding flat pieces of wood.

Their makeshift boats appeared to be propelled by tentacles.

Donovan grinned, and raced over to Airen. He slid an arm around her.

"Looks like our luck has turned, Second Commander."

# CHAPTER EIGHTEEN

Airen leaned heavily on Donovan. She'd torn her injury open again, and the pain made it hard to breathe.

She watched the female warriors run up the beach and into the fight.

Several took on the Kantos. She watched two warriors jump on a turret, hacking it to pieces with their swords.

Across the beach, she met Sanya's gaze. The leader pointed to the prison command building, then inclined her head. Airen nodded back.

"Let's get inside," she said.

Donovan took her hand and together, they dodged the worst of the fighting. The doors to the base were open and a rhythmic clanking noise made them pause.

Several wardens in large mech suits marched out of the base. The ground shuddered under their steps, and the large weapons attached to the shoulders of the suits swiveled to lock on the Kantos. They picked up speed, heading out to join the fight.

Donovan pulled her close to the wall and they pressed against it. She dragged in a breath, fighting back the driving pain. They waited until more wardens in mech suits lumbered out before they both slipped into the base.

Inside was a large courtyard, with smooth, metallic walls and floors. Weapons rested on racks, and there were several vehicles parked in front of what had to be the main entrance to the base.

It was orderly, clean, almost clinical after the rough, wild nature of Oblivion outside the walls.

In the center stood the tower, spearing into the sky, with the landing pad and ship on top.

"We've got to get up that tower," Donovan said.

Airen nodded. They jogged across the courtyard. A second later, she heard the sound of running boots. Wardens were coming.

Donovan tugged her arm, and they ducked in behind a bulky speeder. Rows of wardens ran past them.

Once they were gone, Airen and Donovan jumped up and continued on.

"Hey, you shouldn't be in here," a voice shouted.

They spun and spotted a helmeted warden staring at them.

*Cren.*

Donovan held his hands up. "We just wanted to stay safe." He walked slowly toward the warden.

The prison guard held up a rifle. "No planet inmates are allowed in this facility."

"We aren't inmates," Donovan said.

"They all say that."

Donovan sprang. He hit the warden hard, slamming the man into the speeder. Two more hard punches, and the warden was out cold on the ground.

"There's an elevator at the base of the tower," Airen yelled.

They ran toward it. Alarms started screeching. When they looked back, a huge wave of bugs was pouring through the main doors and into the base.

"Go!" Donovan roared.

They sprinted the rest of the way to the base of the tower. She tried to block the pain, but both she and her helian were running on fumes.

She *had* to keep going. She knew that Donovan wouldn't leave her. Her gorgeous, stubborn mate.

They reached the elevator and she slapped at the control panel. They raced inside and spun. The doors started closing, but the bugs were streaming toward them.

"Come *on*," Donovan muttered.

The doors were almost closed, but one horned bug slammed its head through the gap. It snapped at them, its horn whipping around.

"Doors won't close," she cried.

Donovan moved, swinging his sword at the bug. He sliced its head off, and the doors closed. The elevator moved upward.

She slumped against him and he lifted her chin, kissing her. He gently reached out and touched her bleeding stomach.

"We're going to get off this rock, get you healed, and then I'm going to tan your pretty, white ass."

She stiffened. "Excuse me?"

"Not telling me that we're mated." He gripped her chin. "Or how you feel about me."

"Donovan—"

"You still haven't told me how you feel."

She bit her lip.

"Be brave, Airen. Tell me."

She trembled, fear a horrible thing inside her. He could tear her apart.

"I won't hurt you," he murmured.

She knew that. It resonated in her soul. "I love you, Donovan. My mate."

He grinned and kissed her again. This kiss was hungrier and far deeper.

Suddenly, the elevator jerked to a halt, and they both stumbled.

Spinning, she pressed a palm to the control panel. Nothing happened. She commanded her helian to hack the panel. "The alarms have disabled the elevator."

"Is the ship still on the landing pad?"

She checked the logs and nodded. "They're waiting to evacuate some warden VIPs."

"Well, it's our ride now." Donovan jumped up, grabbing onto a trapdoor that was set in the ceiling of the elevator car.

While he worked on opening it, she accessed the main prison system and hacked into their communications.

Donovan pushed the trap door open and climbed onto the roof of the elevator car. "Come on."

"Wait, I'm going to send an emergency transmission." She quickly sent out an Eon-coded emergency message. She knew they were too far away from Eon space for a warship to pick it up, but maybe there was someone out there who would intercept it. She wanted a record of both her and Donovan's location, in case something happened to them.

She reached up and took his hand. He pulled her onto the top of the elevator car. Long, metallic cables headed upward to the top of the tower.

He gripped the cable and started climbing.

Abdomen aching and fresh blood sliding down her side, she gripped the cable. Then she followed him.

Climbing was agony. Biting her lip, she breathed through her nose. *Hold on, Airen.*

All of a sudden, the cables moved. "Someone's activating the elevator!"

"Climb!" Donovan roared. "Move it."

Hand over hand, she kept climbing, trying to increase her speed. Below them, the elevator car had begun moving upward.

"We're nearly there," he yelled.

Looking up, she saw Donovan had reached some doors. He was trying to pry them open.

*Cren.* The elevator was coming up fast. If they didn't get out, they'd be squashed.

"Donovan, hurry!"

"Got it." The doors parted and he slid through the opening.

*Just a bit more.* Her stomach spasmed and she cried out. *Move, Airen.*

She grabbed the cable above her head and pulled. The car below was picking up speed. She had to move faster.

"Airen, jump!"

She didn't stop to think or reason. She trusted this man completely.

She leaped. Donovan grabbed her and yanked her out through the doorway. The car arrived a second later with a *clang.*

They spilled onto the floor, their hearts pumping. *That was close.*

The elevator doors opened, but the car was empty.

"Damn." Donovan blew out a breath.

They both rose and turned.

They were at the top of the tower. A squat, circular ship was idling on the landing pad. There were no pilots in the cockpit.

"They must have started the engines remotely," she said.

Moving closer, she risked looking over the edge of the pad, and sucked in a sharp breath.

Below, the courtyard was heaving with bugs. She saw a group of wardens with fancy badges and braids on their uniforms, and guessed that they were the VIPs. They were currently being eaten alive.

The prison command was overrun by Kantos.

"Let's get aboard that ship and get off this hellhole." Donovan yanked her toward the ship.

They'd almost reached the ship when a Kantos

swarm ship rose up above the landing pad. Airen cursed, clinging to Donovan.

The ship fired.

Donovan tackled her, pulling her in behind a loader unit. The swarm ship fired again, but it wasn't aiming at them.

The back of the warden ship exploded.

"Ah, fuck," Donovan bit out.

---

DONOVAN BIT DOWN on several more curses. He took in the warden ship, and saw that its engines were toast.

The Kantos swarm ship waited for them to reappear, but a second later it moved off, firing at fighters on the ground.

Airen and Donovan rose. She stared at the burning ship.

*Damn.* He stroked a hand over her hair. He'd wanted to get them free, to get off Oblivion. That plan was ruined now.

She spun. "Interested in killing a lot of Kantos?"

He smiled. "Always."

"Good. I have a plan."

*His woman.* She'd never wallow in despair, or be a victim. She'd always pick herself up and move forward. Donovan knew he'd never have to rescue his mate because she could damn well rescue herself. But he could sure as hell stand with her and help her fight. And he could be her strength at night, when she needed arms to hold her tight.

They both moved toward the damaged ship.

"What's your plan, baby?" he asked.

She reached the side of the ship and a black cord snaked out of her wrist. She plugged into a control panel near the underbelly.

"I'm going to overload the ship's power supply. Then we're going to push it off the tower."

He smiled again. "Make a bomb."

"Yes."

"I like your thinking."

Her gaze turned inward as she worked on the ship's controls. He looked around and his gaze snagged on the loader they'd hidden behind earlier. It was probably used to shift cargo on and off the ships.

Perfect for pushing a starship off the edge of the tower.

He jumped on it and got it going.

Airen stepped away from the ship, and he saw the metal near the engines starting to turn red hot. The loader rumbled as he drove forward. She moved toward him and climbed on the side of the loader.

"Do it," she said.

He drove to the ship and there was a clang as the prongs of the loader hit the hull. The loader's engines growled, and slowly the ship moved, metal scraping across the landing pad.

He kept pushing, gunning the loader engine, until the ship teetered on the edge of the tower landing pad.

Then it fell.

Both he and Airen jumped off the loader. They watched the ship plummet down into the courtyard.

*Boom.*

Donovan grabbed her and pulled her close as a cloud of flames and smoke rose up into the air.

They looked over the edge again.

"Holy hell," he breathed.

The ship had blown out part of the prison command building. Dead and burning bugs littered the entire courtyard.

The battle still raged on the beach.

Then Airen stiffened, and he followed her gaze.

Those damn gorilla-bugs had reappeared. The bulky creatures were racing across the courtyard. They hit the tower base and started climbing up, using their four powerful arms.

There were a lot of them.

*Shit, shit, shit.*

"We need a plan," he said. "We can use the loader to fight them off."

She cupped his cheek, calm and serene. She pressed her lips to his. "I love you, Donovan."

*Damn.* He pressed his forehead to hers. He knew there were too many of the gorilla-bugs, and he and Airen had nowhere to go. "We aren't giving up."

"We won't, but I also wanted to share what was most important. You made me realize how much I kept myself shielded." She smiled. "I've never trusted anyone with all of me before. You opened my eyes to so much more."

He kissed her hard and tugged on her hair.

"You're everything, Airen. You're every dream I've ever wanted all in one beautiful, tough warrior package."

Her smile was worth every ache, pain, and battle.

He dragged in a breath. "You made me realize I was hiding from relationships. One, because I was scared of being hurt like my mom, but mostly, because I was afraid I'd turn into my asshole father."

"You are *so* brave and honorable, Donovan Lennox. Nothing like the man who abandoned you."

"And your parents, for whatever reason they left you, missed out on the greatest gift ever."

She clung to him for a second, then stepped back. "Okay, let's fight."

They both climbed into the loader. He had the engine running just as the first gorilla-bug pulled itself over the edge.

The loader rumbled forward and Donovan accelerated. As the Kantos straightened, he rammed it.

Airen leaped off the vehicle, her sword forming. She started fighting another gorilla-bug that had climbed over the edge.

More and more gorilla-bugs pulled themselves up onto the landing pad. Donovan rammed into another one.

There were just too many.

He saw four converge on Airen all at once. *No.* He spun, driving toward her. "Airen!"

*Bang.* The loader vibrated. Looking up, he saw a gorilla-bug on the steel cage that formed the loader's roof, staring down at him.

*Oh, shit.*

Suddenly, a deafening roar of sound cut through the air.

Donovan looked up. *Oh, hell.*

There was a ship in the sky. A big one.

And it wasn't Eon, Terran, or Kantos.

The ship was black, sleek and angular, with huge, spiked plates of metal on its hull, almost like armor. Its engines glowed blue.

The gorilla-bugs froze. The large ship started firing blue energy pulses toward the beach.

The gorilla-bugs pulled back, disappearing over the edge of the tower. Retreating.

Airen ran toward Donovan, beaming. He leaped off the loader and was just in time to catch her. She jumped on him, legs wrapping around his waist. Then she kissed him hard.

"I take it that's a friend?" he asked.

"Yes." Her smile widened. "That's an Oronis ship."

*Oronis.* Jamie Park, one of the *Divergent's* space marines, and her warrior mate, Aydin, had been helped by an Oronis spy. The man had saved them from the Kantos.

"A related species to the Eon, right?"

"The Oronis knights are fierce fighters."

As she spoke, he watched a wave of black bodies pour out of the Oronis ship.

The fighters flew closer—all wearing kickass, black armor, three-quarter coats flaring behind them. Their heads were covered by black helmets. He couldn't see any wing suits or anything, but the knights landed in crouches across the beach.

Then, they unleashed hell.

In awe, Donovan watched several knights draw long swords that glittered with blue energy. Others formed blue balls of energy between their gloved palms.

If the Eon warriors were strong, tough broadswords, the Oronis were sleek, deadly rapiers. Across the beach, the knights fought with lethal intensity. Donovan watched a blue ball of energy hit a Kantos soldier. The Kantos writhed, the energy racing over it, before it burned up to a husk.

He hugged Airen closer. "I like your friends."

## CHAPTER NINETEEN

A iren and Donovan stepped out of the elevator. Dead Kantos and wardens covered the courtyard, but it was the Oronis who dominated Airen's attention.

A group of the knights stood nearby, identical in their black armor and sleek visors.

One raised his head and looked at them before striding their way, his coat flaring out behind him.

Donovan's arm tightened around her.

*Cren*, she was exhausted. Her overworked helian was trying to heal both her and Donovan's injuries. She wanted to climb into bed and sleep for a week.

The knight's visor retracted, revealing a sharply handsome face, with a hawkish nose and rather sensuous lips. The man's eyes were a startling blue, like a web of cracks. He had space-black hair, far shorter than Eon warriors, but longer than Donovan's. It was long enough to curl at the collar of his black armor.

She inclined her head. "Knightmaster."

"Second Commander Kann-Felis." His voice was deep and resonant. "Sub-Captain Lennox."

Her head shot up. "You know who we are?"

The knightmaster gave her a sharp nod. "War Commander Dann-Jad tasked us to rescue you. They determined a wormhole had transported your shuttle, and with some enhanced technology, managed to calculate your approximate location. My ship, the *BlackBlade*, was closest."

"Thanks," Donovan said. "We couldn't have held out much longer."

"We picked up the emergency transmission you sent, although we were already tracking the Kantos activity to this location." The knightmaster's face didn't change, but Airen detected his disdain for the Kantos.

"Appreciate it." Donovan held out a hand. "I'm Donovan Lennox."

The Oronis took his hand. "Knightmaster Ashtin." His gaze ran over them. "You are both injured. Allow the knighthealers aboard my ship to tend to you."

Airen nodded, just as her legs gave out.

"I've got you, Second Commander." Donovan swept his arms around her and lifted her off her feet.

He did. She trusted now that he always would. But old fears were still there, nibbling inside her. No one had valued her long enough to keep her forever. Not even her own parents. Would Donovan move on when things got routine?

They strode out of the prison command base.

"Knightmaster Ashtin, the residents of this planet assisted us in the fight," she said.

He nodded. "They have suffered a few casualties, but it appears local fauna in the water assisted them."

"Could you return them to their base? Get them some supplies?"

"Consider it done."

A black shuttle had landed nearby. Donovan followed the knightmaster aboard, settling them both into a large black seat. Soon, they were taking off, heading toward the Oronis ship.

"This rocks," Donovan murmured appreciatively.

"The Oronis and Eon share a lot of technology," she said. "Although, they do have a grander sense of style than the Eon."

Once they'd docked, they stepped aboard the Oronis cruiser. Inside, the walls were dark and sleek. Lighting consisted of a bright-blue color. It was more ornate than an Eon ship, with its arched doorways, and carved, metal walls.

When they entered Medical, they were welcomed by a female knighthealer, also wearing black armor, and no less deadly-looking than the rest of the knights they'd seen.

"Over here, please. I'm Knighthealer Taera."

Airen stretched out on the bunk and the woman's hands glowed blue. She moved them over Airen's wounds and she felt a burning in her stomach. She gritted her teeth.

Donovan leaned close, his hand clasping hers.

"Do they have helians?" he asked quietly.

"No. They have something else."

The knighthealer moved away to confer with some of

her team, and then returned. "Your injuries are healing well, but you require rest."

"Can you check Donovan?" Airen asked.

He shook his head. "No need. My injuries were all minor, and your helian's already fixed me up. Just a few aches and bruises left."

The knighthealer raised a palm and the center of it glowed blue. "He is correct. I suggest some rest for you as well, Sub-Captain. The knightmaster has assigned you quarters. You can sleep and rest until we rendezvous with your ship in a few hours."

"So soon?" Airen asked.

"Once they contacted us about your location, I believe your ship has made several star jumps to reach us."

That sounded like Malax. He would never abandon any of his warriors.

"Thank you, Knighthealer."

The woman smiled and inclined her head.

A young knight showed Airen and Donovan to a spacious cabin. The walls were similarly black and gleaming, and less-intense blue lighting lit the room. A large bed was topped with a black cover, and a tray of food rested on a long, narrow side table.

"I need to be clean," she said.

Donovan helped her into the adjoining washroom. Panels of blue lit up the space, and soon, he had hot water going in the shower.

She stripped off her clothes and stepped under the spray. She moaned at the pleasure.

A second later, Donovan slipped in behind her,

naked. His big hands moved up over her breasts, and she moaned again.

"Now I plan to punish you, my mate, for trying to hide our mating."

She watched his dark hand slide down her belly and between her legs. She moaned his name. His clever fingers got busy, caressing, stroking, teasing.

His mouth nipped at her ear. "I'm gonna make you come. Again, again, and again, baby."

Her mate was true to his word. He brought her to the brink again and again, one hand between her legs while the other moved up to cup her breast, then down again.

"*Donovan,*" she moaned.

"Punishment. My warrior mate needs to trust her man."

Finally, a thick finger slid inside her, his thumb on her clit. It didn't take much. Airen came hard, only Donovan's strength keeping her upright.

Then he scooped her up and turned off the shower. He carried her to the bed, uncaring that they were both still wet.

As he laid her out, she saw the light in his eyes.

"I am damn glad we made it, Airen."

He pressed a kiss to her lips before his mouth wandered lower, gently kissing the knitting wound on her stomach. Her man could be so gentle.

"I'm damn glad you're mine." Then his mouth was on hers again. "Not going to let you go."

She wrapped her arms around him, but a voice inside her head warned that soon they'd return to their ships. To their careers, duties and responsibilities.

But then Donovan slid inside her, and she couldn't think of anything but him.

---

MAN, the Oronis ship kicked ass.

Donovan had never been on a bridge so slick. The comm stations were all transparent, black screens manned by Oronis knights.

Airen stood beside him. After a few hours of rest and some food, her color was better, and she was back in pure-warrior mode—armor on, posture straight, her brown hair braided.

There was no sign of the touch-hungry woman he'd held in his arms the last few hours.

When she glanced up at him, she gave him a small smile, but he sensed something was bothering her.

"The *Rengard* is in range," a knight called out.

Knightmaster Ashtin nodded.

The *Rengard* appeared on the viewscreen, and Donovan felt a stab of relief.

*They'd made it.*

Even better, the Kantos had suffered another blow.

It wasn't long before the *BlackBlade* docked with the *Rengard*.

"Thank you again." Donovan shook hands with the knightmaster.

"The Kantos are our enemy too. Good luck in your fight, and know that we are here if you need our assistance."

The knightmaster and several of his knights walked

them to the airlock. When the door opened, Donovan saw a crowd waiting for them.

"Donovan!" Wren engulfed him in a hug. Malax pulled Airen close, and Sabin rested a hand on her shoulder.

"Well, you look nice in your Eon armor." Wren grinned at Donovan, her gaze sliding down the black-scales covering his body.

"You aren't the only one who found yourself an Eon mate." He pulled Airen away from the other warriors, settling her under his arm.

"Well." Malax nodded. "I'm very happy for both of you."

"We were so shocked that the Kantos had manipulated a wormhole and took you," Wren said. "Sassy and I worked overtime to find you."

"Thank you, Wren," Airen said.

"We did like three years of wormhole research in one day, and Malax has been utilizing the helian-tech aboard the *Rengard* to get us here ASAP. We weren't letting the Kantos have you guys." Wren lowered her voice. "Plus, Malax is a grump without you, Airen. He says you're the best second commander he's ever had."

Donovan saw the pride in his mate's face and stroked her braid.

Thane pushed forward. The silver-haired medical commander was frowning. "You're both injured. I want you in Medical, now."

Airen turned. "Thane, I'm fine—"

"I'm the medical commander aboard the ship," the man said in a firm, unyielding tone.

"You can be very bossy, Thane," she grumbled.

"My job, especially when dealing with stubborn warriors."

Donovan urged her on. "Listen to your medical commander." He wouldn't mind having her checked over, as well.

"I need to check you, too, Sub-Captain."

"Ah—"

"Listen to the medical commander," Airen said.

He swatted her ass out of view of the others, and she smiled.

In Medical, they were both hooked up to several scanners. Donovan watched as Thane checked Airen's healing wounds.

"Everything is healing well, if a little slow. You need rest, and an intake of nutrients."

Airen sat up. "I need to debrief my team. I need to—"

"Lie down and rest," Donovan said with a growl. "We've been abducted, held captive, hunted, attacked, almost drowned, injured—"

"Okay, okay," she muttered.

Then a scanner beeped and Thane moved. With a frown, he touched Donovan's thigh.

Donovan frowned. "Problem?"

"There's some debris under your skin. It's likely nothing dangerous, but I'll need to remove it."

"What?" Airen pushed off the bed and moved closer, looking a little panicked. "Could this hurt him? What if—?"

Donovan cupped her head and pulled her close. He

kissed her until she was breathless. "Lie down or I'll make you lie down."

She glared at him, but reluctantly sat on the bunk beside his.

"I need to put you under," Thane said.

Donovan nodded and lay down. Airen reached out and took his hand.

It was nice to have her there. "Watch over me?"

She stroked his hair. "Yes."

"You trusting this yet? Me? Our mating?"

Something flashed in her eyes.

"Baby?" Worry hit him. Was this not what she wanted? He felt the pressure injector at his thigh. "Wait—"

But already his vision was blurring, darkness sucking him under.

The last thing he saw was Airen's concerned face.

## CHAPTER TWENTY

Every muscle in Airen's body stayed tense until Thane completed Donovan's medical procedure.

"He'll be fine," the medical commander said. "He's extremely fit and healthy."

She nodded, stroking Donovan's hair.

"Congratulations on your mating, Airen."

She glanced up at Thane. "You've never found your mate?"

He shook his head. "You know it's rare these days for the Eon. Although, it seems the Terrans are changing that."

"Do you want a mate?"

A small smile touched the medical commander's lips. "I'm mated to my work." He tilted his head, his gaze on her. "Did you want a mate?"

"I never imagined it would happen." She stared at Donovan's strong, handsome face. The even rise and fall of his broad chest.

"You're unhappy?" Thane said carefully.

"I love him so much it leaves me breathless. He's a good, honorable man."

"But?" Thane prodded.

"I'm Eon, he's Terran. We both have command careers in different fleets." She stood. "I need to get to the bridge."

Thane scowled. "You need rest and time to recover."

"I'm fine. I promise I won't push myself. Watch over him?"

"Of course."

When Airen strode onto the bridge, she saw Malax and Sabin at the light table, locked in an intense conversation. Wren was slumped in a chair. The entire bridge felt tense.

When Malax saw her, his brows drew together. "You should be in Medical."

"I'm perfectly healthy." She glanced at their set faces. She'd worked with these men long enough to know how to read them. "What's wrong?"

"Is Donovan awake?" Malax asked.

"Not yet. What's happened?" Worry gripped her. "Were other female warriors attacked?"

Malax shook his head. "You were the female warrior closest to the edge of Eon space, the easiest target." His lips quirked. "Clearly a bad assumption by the Kantos. After you were taken, we warned all other ships with female warriors aboard."

Airen glanced at Wren and saw the woman had been crying. She looked back at Malax. "So what's wrong?"

Sabin straightened. "The Kantos attacked Earth."

"What?" Airen took a step closer.

"A minor incursion," Sabin said. "Likely, they were checking the planet's defenses. They attacked the city of Houston, where Space Corps headquarters is located."

"The Terrans activated an experimental weapon system," Malax said.

Sabin nodded. "They destroyed the Kantos ship."

"The Kantos will try again," Airen said. "They're going after the weakest link. They had no luck attacking Eon ships and trying to get our helians. Now, they'll go after the Terrans."

Malax nodded, moving to place his hands on Wren's shoulders. The Terran woman leaned into her mate. "They'll attack man, woman, and child. They don't care who they destroy."

"They're also testing our alliance," she mused. "To see just how far the Eon will go to protect the Terrans."

"We have a call from the king coming in shortly," Malax said. "We need to discuss our next steps."

"Good, I—"

The bridge doors opened, and an angry Donovan strode in. His long legs quickly covered the distance between them.

"You're supposed to be resting in Medical," he bit out.

She lifted a hand. "Donovan—"

He didn't wait to hear what she had to say. He yanked her into his arms and kissed her. It didn't take much for her to melt into him. She kissed him back, hot

209

and hard. She felt the solid thump of his heart under her palm. He was alive, and she was so grateful for that.

"Malax, is there a reason your second commander and the sub-captain are kissing on your bridge?" a deep, authoritative, highly amused voice said.

She froze. *Oh, cren.*

She pressed her head against Donovan's chest.

"Who's that?" he murmured.

"The king of the Eon Empire."

Female laughter came across the comm line. "I can't send you anywhere, Lennox."

They both looked up.

Two faces were on the screen. The left side showed the ruler of the Eon, King Gayel Solann-Eon. The man wore a faint smile on his handsome, rugged face. He had the typical long, brown hair of an Eon warrior, and wore a sleeveless shirt in a rich blue. A gold cord circled one of his muscled biceps.

The second image was of Donovan's captain, Allie Borden. The blonde Terran wore a crisp Space Corps uniform, and was grinning.

Malax stepped forward. "Actually, they have a very good reason, Gayel. Airen and Donovan are mated."

"Donovan." Allie shook her head, surprise on her face. "Congratulations."

Donovan pulled Airen close to his side. "Thanks."

King Gayel inclined his head. "Yet another mating. I'm very happy for you both."

"Thank you, your Majesty," Airen said.

The king's smile faded. "Unfortunately, we have less

happy news to talk about. And I'm very sorry to hear about your ordeal with the Kantos."

"Luckily, Donovan and I were together." She glanced at her mate. "I doubt I would have survived without him."

"Ditto," Donovan murmured. "Sir, the Kantos need a stronger warning. They came after Airen and her helian."

She gripped his arm. "Donovan, there's more."

He frowned. "What's happened?"

It was Allie who answered. "D, the Kantos attacked Earth."

He cursed. "Casualties?"

"Thankfully, quite small." The anger in her voice said that even one loss was too many. "It wasn't a full-scale attack. More like a small strike team that attacked Houston."

Airen watched a muscle in Donovan's jaw tick.

"Testing our capabilities," he said.

All the warriors around them nodded.

"We will *not* allow the Kantos to destroy Earth," King Gayel said. "I've authorized a small team of Eon warriors to be assigned to Earth."

Airen's eyes widened, and Donovan squeezed her hand.

"The plan is for them to work with our defense team," Allie said. "Help in designing experimental weapons for planetary defense."

"We need to send our best weapons experts," Gayel continued. "Malax, I'd like to borrow your security commander."

Airen glanced at Sabin. His work before the *Rengard* had included advanced weapons technology.

The warrior straightened and nodded. "I'll do whatever my king and war commander order."

"Good," the king said. "I'm told that you will work with the head of the Terran weapons projects. A Dr. Finley Delgado."

"Oh," Wren whispered from nearby.

"What?" Airen asked.

"Let's just say Dr. Delgado is smarter than me, and is known to be...temperamental. She's very good at what she does, she just doesn't play well with others."

"She?" Airen said.

"Should be interesting," Donovan murmured.

Suddenly, Airen felt a flash of heat through her entire body. Her cheeks felt like they were on fire. She gripped Donovan's hand, her legs feeling weak.

He frowned at her. "What's wrong, Airen?"

She gritted her teeth, drawing in his scent. *Just hold it together until the king is finished, Airen.*

Wren smiled at Donovan, and Airen growled at the woman. She had her own mate. She didn't need to smile at Airen's, or stand so close to him.

Donovan frowned. Acting purely on instinct, Airen reached up and kissed him. She didn't care about their audience; she *needed* her mate.

The king coughed, clearly hiding a laugh.

When Airen looked up and blinked, Malax was smiling. "Go."

Airen grabbed Donovan's hand and dragged her confused mate off the bridge.

"Airen, what is going on?"

"Mating fever."

His scowl morphed into a sexy grin. "My cabin or yours?"

---

## Sabin

SABIN SOLANN-ATH SAT at the desk in the conference room off the bridge.

He was interested to see Earth, and had already packed for his assignment. Weaponry was his area of expertise. If he could help take down the Kantos and protect Earth, it was his duty as an Eon warrior.

Sabin had given a lot in service to his Empire. He was a warrior to the bone. A honed weapon. He liked order, and he liked challenges.

He didn't think Earth would provide much in the way of a challenge, but at least he could help.

He waited for the call to connect to Earth. He was to make contact with the Terran scientist in charge of the weapons project, Dr. Finley Delgado.

The call connected to show an empty room.

He frowned. "Hello?" He'd made the call exactly at the assigned time.

Someone walked past the camera and sat. "What do you want?"

Sabin blinked at the sharp, female voice. He hadn't realized the scientist was a woman.

A beautiful woman.

She was tall, with curves, and long, blonde-brown hair pinned up at the back of her head. She had a regal-looking face, with high cheekbones. And brown eyes that looked annoyed.

"I am Security Commander Sabin Solann-Ath of the Eon warship, the *Rengard*. Are you Dr. Delgado?"

She tucked a strand of hair back behind her ear with a quick flick of her wrist. "Yes. And I'm busy. I have an important project that needs my attention. I don't have time for an intergalactic chitchat."

The clipped voice told Sabin that this woman was not very patient.

He dragged in a breath, trying to find his own patience. "I've been assigned to assist you. I—"

Dr. Delgado leaned forward and actually looked at him. Or rather his arms.

She frowned. "I don't see what use I have for a brawny alien warrior."

Sabin sucked in a breath. She was insulting him?

She waved a slim hand. It was stained with something. Old-fashioned ink, maybe. "The Kantos could attack at any minute and I have to be ready. I *have* to stop them." It was the first time he'd heard any sort of emotion in her voice.

"And I'll be helping you do that, Dr. Delgado."

Her nose wrinkled. "I don't need help."

"You want all the glory for yourself, so you ignore others who could help you?" He detested people who worked for fame and glory, instead of honor and integrity.

Her brown eyes widened. "What? No. I want to be left alone to concentrate, Commander Brawn."

He crossed his arms over his chest. *Infuriating female.* But warrior that he was, he noted the way her gaze snagged on his crossed arms. "My name is Security Commander Sabin Solann-Ath."

The scientist blinked and shook her head. "I don't need your help."

"Well, you're getting it. I'll arrive in three days."

Dr. Delgado huffed and touched something. The screen went blank.

She'd *ended* the call.

Sabin ground his teeth together. He liked and respected the Terrans he'd met so far. It appeared Dr. Finley Delgado wouldn't be earning his respect anytime soon, but he would still carry out his duty.

---

*JESUS.*

Donovan's body arched up, and he blindly grabbed Airen's hips.

She was riding him, hard, her face flushed and her hair loose and tangled.

"*Donovan*," she moaned.

He felt that she was close and thumbed her clit. "Get there, sexy girl. Let me see you come."

Her hips moved faster and she moaned again. With another thrust of her hips, she splintered apart, her body clenching on his cock.

God, he *never* got tired of watching her find her pleasure. Her husky cries were music to his ears.

Her climax triggered his own. He sat up and spun her flat on her back. He thrust back inside her, pistoning into her tight body.

She cried out, her legs clamping onto him, heels digging into his ass.

Donovan groaned, pumping inside her. His release was a roar of sound and sensation.

Spent, he rolled off her, dropping beside her on the bed.

The bed—no, the entire cabin—was a mess. They hadn't constrained their love-making to the bed. He'd had her in the shower, against the wall, on the desk, on the floor, on the chair.

He was tired, but he felt awesome. He guessed two days straight of sex would do that.

Airen shifted and pressed in close.

"Well, mating fever rocks," he said, finally.

She laughed.

He loved that sound. "So, are you going to make room for my stuff in your closet?"

She raised her head, an unreadable look in her black-green eyes.

He cupped her cheek. "I'm moving in, Airen. I love you, and you love me. That's what people who love each other do."

She licked her lips, and he instantly felt that small move in his cock.

"You are so damn beautiful," he whispered.

But she pulled away and sat up, a serious look on her face. Donovan frowned.

"We come from different worlds, Donovan," she said carefully. "We're both dedicated to our careers."

"Uh-huh." He sat up as well.

"I'm Eon, you're with Space Corps—"

He tumbled her under him. After all the loving, after everything they'd shared, she still doubted him.

No, not him. Every single event in her life had left her wary of truly opening up and trusting her heart. He knew that.

"Airen—"

"You're amazing, Donovan. I know you probably want to captain your own ship one day, and you'd be a brilliant captain. I don't know how we can be together and make this work."

He cupped both her cheeks. "Listen to me. We took on pirates, criminals, genetically engineered creatures, Kantos...if we can do all that, we can sort out anything."

"I don't want you to compromise, and one day, wake up resenting us—"

"*Anything*. Together."

He saw the flare of hope in her black-green eyes. She wanted to believe.

"Do you love me?" he demanded.

She dragged in a shaky breath.

"Be brave," he said. "Trust me."

"Yes. I love you so much, Donovan."

He kissed her, taking his time to nibble on her lips. "We'll sort it all out. For now, we're both on the *Rengard*. And what I want is my beautiful, competent, sexy warrior-mate by my side. Always. I'm right where I want to be, Airen."

She trembled. "I love you."

"I know. I claimed you, my warrior. I hunted you

down and claimed you, fair and square. You were naked, I fought off rabid criminals..."

She rolled her eyes. "I think I fought off more criminals."

"Nothing you can do can change the fact that you're mine, Airen Kann-Felis, just as I'm yours."

"And we can take on anything together," she whispered.

"Hell, yeah. We come up against any problem, any enemy, more Kantos, I'm sending you in to fight." He nipped her lips. "I love watching my warrior kick ass. And I love your ass, and your legs, and your—"

Laughing, she kissed him. "I think I get it."

"That," he whispered. "That laugh. I'm going to spend the rest of our lives making you laugh, Airen. Making you feel loved."

Then he kissed his mate, and set about loving her all over again.

---

I hope you enjoyed Airen and Donovan's story!

Eon Warriors continues with *Storm of Eon* starring Security Commander Sabin Solann-Ath and Dr. Finley Delgado. Coming in 2021.

For more action-packed romance, read on for a preview of the first chapter of *Gladiator,* the first book in my best-selling Galactic Gladiators series.

**Don't miss out!** For updates about new releases, action romance info, free books, and other fun stuff, sign up for my VIP mailing list and get your *free box set* containing three action-packed romances.

Visit here to get started: www.annahackett.com

Would you like
a FREE BOX SET
of my books?

# PREVIEW: GLADIATOR

## MORE SCI-FI ROMANCE

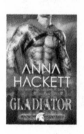

**Fighting for love, honor, and freedom on the galaxy's lawless outer rim.**

*Fighting for love, honor, and freedom on the galaxy's lawless outer rim...*

*When Earth space marine Harper Adams finds herself abducted by alien slavers off a space station, her life turns into a battle for survival. Dumped into an arena on a desert planet on the outer rim, she finds herself face to face with a big, tattooed alien gladiator...the champion of the Kor Magna Arena.*

Just another day at the office.

Harper Adams pulled herself along the outside of the space station module. She could hear her quiet breathing inside her spacesuit, and she easily pulled her weightless body along the slick, white surface of the module. She stopped to check a security panel, ensuring all the systems were running smoothly.

*Check.* Same as it had been yesterday, and the day before that. But Harper never ever let herself forget that they were six hundred million kilometers away from Earth. That meant they were dependent only on themselves. She tapped some buttons on the security panel before closing the reinforced plastic cover. She liked to dot all her *I*s and cross all her *T*s. She never left anything to chance.

She grabbed the handholds and started pulling herself up over the cylindrical pod to check the panels on the other side. Glancing back behind herself, she caught a beautiful view of the planet below.

Harper stopped and made herself take it all in. The orange, white, and cream bands of Jupiter could take your breath away. Today, she could even see the famous superstorm of the Great Red Spot. She'd been on the Fortuna Research Station for almost eighteen months. That meant, despite the amazing view, she really didn't see it anymore.

She turned her head and looked down the length of the space station. At the end was the giant circular donut that housed the main living quarters and offices. The main ring rotated to provide artificial gravity for the residents. Lying off the center of the ring was the long cylinder of the research facility, and off that cylinder were several modules that housed various scientific labs and storage. At the far end of the station was the docking area for the supply ships that came from Earth every few months.

"Lieutenant Adams? Have you finished those checks?"

Harper heard the calm voice of her fellow space marine and boss, Captain Samantha Santos, through the comm system in her helmet.

"Almost done," Harper answered.

"Take a good look at the botany module. The computer's showing some strange energy spikes, but the scientists in there said everything looks fine. Must be a system malfunction."

Which meant the geek squad engineers were going to have to come in and do some maintenance. "On it."

Harper swung her body around, and went feet-first down the other side of the module. She knew the rest of the security team—all made up of United Nations Space Marines—would be running similar checks on the other modules across the station. They had a great team to ensure the safety of the hundreds of scientists aboard the station. There was also a dedicated team of engineers that kept the guts of the station running.

She passed a large, solid window into the module, and could see various scientists floating around benches filled with all kinds of plants. They all wore matching gray jumpsuits accented with bright-blue at the collars, that indicated science team. There was a vast mix of scientists and disciplines aboard—biologists, botanists, chemists, astronomers, physicists, medical experts, and the list went on. All of them were conducting experiments, and some were searching for alien life beyond the edge of the solar system. It seemed like every other week, more probes were being sent out to hunt for radio signals or collect samples.

Since humans had perfected large solar sails as a way to safely and quickly propel spacecraft, getting around the solar system had become a lot easier. With radiation pressure exerted by sunlight onto the mirrored sails, they could travel from Earth to Fortuna Station orbiting Jupiter in just a few months. And many of the scientists aboard the station were looking beyond the solar system, planning manned expeditions farther and farther away. Harper wasn't sure they were quite ready for that.

She quickly checked the adjacent control panel. Among all the green lights, she spotted one that was blinking red, and she frowned. They definitely had a problem with the locking system on the exterior door at the end of the module. She activated the small propulsion pack on her spacesuit, and circled around the module. She slowed down as she passed the large, round exterior door at the end of the cylindrical module.

It was all locked into place and looked secure.

As she moved back to the module, she grabbed a handhold and then tapped the small tablet attached to the forearm of her suit. She keyed in a request for maintenance to come and check it.

She looked up and realized she was right near

another window. Through the reinforced glass, a pretty, curvy blonde woman looked up and spotted Harper. She smiled and waved. Harper couldn't help but smile and lifted her gloved hand in greeting.

Dr. Regan Forrest was a botanist and a few years younger than Harper. The young woman was so open and friendly, and had befriended Harper from her first day on the station. Harper had never had a lot of friends —mainly because she'd been too busy raising her younger sister and working. She'd never had time for girly nights out or gossip.

But Regan was friendly, smart, and had the heart of a steamroller under her pretty exterior. Harper always had trouble saying no to her. Maybe the woman reminded her a little of Brianna. At the thought of her sister, something twisted painfully in Harper's chest.

Regan floated over to the window and held up a small tablet. She'd typed in some words.

*Cards tonight?*

Harper had been teaching Regan how to play poker. The woman was terrible at it, and Harper beat her all the time. But Regan never gave up.

Harper nodded and held up two fingers to indicate a couple of hours. She was off-shift shortly, and then she had a sparring match with Regan's cousin, Rory—one of the station engineers—in the gym. Aurora "Call me Rory or I'll hit you" Fraser had been trained in mixed martial arts, and Harper found the female engineer a hell of a sparring partner. Rory was teaching Harper some martial arts moves and Harper was showing the woman some basic sword moves. Since she was little, Harper had been a keen fencer.

Regan grinned back and nodded. Then the woman's wide smile disappeared. She spun around, and through the glass Harper could see the other scientists all looking around, concerned. One scientist was spinning around, green plants floating in the air around him, along with fat droplets of water and some other green fluid. He'd clearly screwed up and let his experiment get free.

"Lieutenant Adams?" The captain's voice came through her helmet again. "Harper?"

There was a sense of urgency that made Harper's belly tighten. "Go ahead, Captain."

"We have an alarm sounding in the botany module. The computer says there is a risk of decompression."

*Dammit.* "I just checked the security panels. The locking mechanism on the exterior door is showing red. I did a visual inspection and it's closed up tight."

"Okay, we talked with the scientist in charge. Looks like one of her team let something loose in there. It isn't dangerous, but it must be messing with the alarm sensors. System's locked them all in there." She made an annoyed sound. "Idiots will have to stay there until engineering can get down there and free them."

Harper studied the room through the glass again. Some of the green liquid had floated over to another bench that contained various frothing cylinders on it. A second later, the cylinders shattered, their contents bubbling upward.

The scientists all moved to the back exit of the

module, banging on the locked door. *Damn.* They were trapped.

Harper met Regan's gaze. Her friend's face was pale, and wisps of her blonde hair had escaped her ponytail, floating around her face.

"Captain," Harper said. "Something's wrong. The experiments have overflowed their containment." She could see the scientists were all coughing.

"Engineering is on the way," the captain said.

Harper pushed herself off, flying over the surface of the module. She reached the control panel and saw that several other lights had turned red. They needed to get this under control and they needed to do it now.

"Harper!" The captain's panicked voice. "Decompression in progress!"

*What the hell?* The module jerked beneath Harper. She looked up and saw the exterior door blow off, flying away from the station.

Her heart stopped. That meant all the scientists were exposed to the vacuum of space.

*Fuck.* Harper pushed off again, sending herself flying toward the end of the module. She put her arms by her sides to help increase her speed. Through the window, she saw that most of the scientists had grabbed on to whatever they could hold on to. A few were pulling emergency breathers over their heads.

She reached the end of the pod and saw the damage. There was torn metal where the door had been ripped off. Inside the door, she knew there would be a temporary repair kit containing a sheet of high-tech nano fabric that could be stretched across the opening to reestablish pressure. But it needed to be put in place manually. Harper reached for the latch to release the repair kit.

Suddenly, a slim body shot out of the pod, her arms and legs kicking. Her mouth was wide open in a silent scream.

*Regan.* Harper didn't let herself think. She turned, pushed off and fired her propulsion system, arrowing after her friend.

"Security Team to the botany module," she yelled through her comm system. "Security Team to botany module. We have decompression. One scientist has been expelled. I'm going after her. I need someone that can help calm the others and get the module sealed again."

"Acknowledged, Lieutenant," Captain Santos answered. "I'm on my way."

Harper focused on reaching Regan. She was gaining on her. She saw that the woman had lost consciousness. She also knew that Regan had only a couple of minutes to survive out here. Harper let her training take over. She tapped the propulsion system controls, trying for more speed, as she maneuvered her way toward Regan.

As she got close, Harper reached out and wrapped her arm around the scientist. "I've got you."

Harper turned, at the same time clipping a safety line to the loops on Regan's jumpsuit. Then, she touched the controls and propelled them straight back towards the module. She kept her friend pulled tightly toward her chest. *Hold on, Regan.*

She was so still. It reminded Harper of holding Brianna's dead body in her arms. Harper's jaw tightened. She wouldn't let Regan die out here. The woman had dreamed of working in space, and worked her entire career to get here, even defying her family. Harper wasn't going to fail her.

As the module got closer, she saw that the security team had arrived. She saw the captain's long, muscled body as she and another man put up the nano fabric.

"Incoming. Keep the door open."

"Can't keep it open much longer, Adams," the captain replied. "Make it snappy."

Harper adjusted her course, and, a second later, she shot through the door with Regan in her arms. Behind her, the captain and another huge security marine, Lieutenant Blaine Strong, pulled the stretchy fabric across the opening.

"Decompression contained," the computer intoned.

Harper released a breath. On the panel beside the door, she saw the lights turning green. The nano fabric wouldn't hold forever, but it would do until they got everyone out of here, and then got a maintenance team in here to fix the door.

"Oxygen levels at required levels," the computer said again.

"Good work, Lieutenant." Captain Sam Santos floated over. She was a tall woman with a strong face and brown hair she kept pulled back in a tight ponytail. She had curves she kept ruthlessly toned, and golden skin she always said was thanks to her Puerto Rican heritage.

"Thanks, Captain." Harper ripped her helmet off and looked down at Regan.

Her blonde hair was a wild tangle, her face was pale and marked by what everyone who worked in space

229

called space hickeys—bruises caused by the skin's small blood vessels bursting when exposed to the vacuum of space. *Please be okay.*

"Here." Blaine appeared, holding a portable breather. The big man was an excellent marine. He was about six foot five with broad shoulders that stretched his spacesuit to the limit. She knew he was a few inches over the height limit for space operations, but he was a damn good marine, which must have gone in his favor. He had dark skin thanks to his African-American father and his handsome face made him popular with the station's single ladies, but mostly he worked and hung out with the other marines.

"Thanks." Harper slipped the clear mask over Regan's mouth.

"Nice work out there." Blaine patted her shoulder. "She's alive because of you."

Suddenly, Regan jerked, pulling in a hard breath.

"You're okay." Harper gripped Regan's shoulder. "Take it easy."

Regan looked around the module, dazed and panicky. Harper watched as Regan caught sight of the fabric stretched across the end of the module, and all the plants floating around inside.

"God," Regan said with a raspy gasp, her breath fogging up the dome of the breather. She shook her head, her gaze moving to Harper. "Thanks, Harper."

"Any time." Harper squeezed her friend's shoulder. "It's what I'm here for."

Regan managed a wan smile. "No, it's just you. You

didn't have to fly out into space to rescue me. I'm grateful."

"Come on. We need to get you to the infirmary so they can check you out. Maybe put some cream on your hickeys."

"Hickeys?" Regan touched her face and groaned. "Oh, no. I'm going to get a ribbing."

"And you didn't even get them the pleasurable way."

A faint blush touched Regan's cheeks. "That's right. If I had, at least the ribbing would have been worth it."

With a relieved laugh, Harper looked over at her captain. "I'm going to get Regan to the infirmary."

The other woman nodded. "Good. We'll meet you back at the Security Center."

With a nod, Harper pushed off, keeping one arm around Regan, and they floated into the main part of the science facility. Soon, they moved through the entrance into the central hub of the space station. As the artificial gravity hit, Harper's boots thudded onto the floor. Beside her, Regan almost collapsed.

Harper took most of the woman's weight and helped her down the corridor. They pushed into the infirmary.

A gray-haired, barrel-chested man rushed over. "Decided to take an unscheduled spacewalk, Dr. Forrest?"

Regan smiled weakly. "Yes. Without a spacesuit."

The doctor made a tsking sound and then took her from Harper. "We'll get her all patched up."

Harper nodded. "I'll come and check on you later."

Regan grabbed her hand. "We have a blackjack game

231

scheduled. I'm planning to win back all those chocolates you won off me."

Harper snorted. "You can try." It was good to see some life back in Regan's blue eyes.

As Harper strode out into the corridor, she ran a hand through her dark hair, tension slowly melting out of her shoulders. She really needed a beer. She tilted her neck one way and then the other, hearing the bones pop.

*Just another day at the office.* The image of Regan drifting away from the space station burst in her head. Harper released a breath. She was okay. Regan was safe and alive. That was all that mattered.

With a shake of her head, Harper headed toward the Security Center. She needed to debrief with the captain and clock off. Then she could get out of her spacesuit and take the one-minute shower that they were all allotted.

That was the one thing she missed about Earth. Long, hot showers.

And swimming. She'd been a swimmer all her life and there were days she missed slicing through the water.

She walked along a long corridor, meeting a few people—mainly scientists. She reached a spot where there was a long bank of windows that afforded a lovely view of Jupiter, and space beyond it.

Stingy showers and unscheduled spacewalks aside, Harper had zero regrets about coming out into space. There'd been nothing left for her on Earth, and to her surprise, she'd made friends here on Fortuna.

As she stared out into the black, mesmerized by the twinkle of stars, she caught a small flash of light in the distance. She paused, frowning. What the hell was that?

She stared hard at the spot where she'd seen the flash. Nothing there but the pretty sprinkle of stars. Harper shook her head. Fatigue was playing tricks on her. It had to have just been a weird trick of the lights reflecting off the glass.

Pushing the strange sighting away, she continued on to the Security Center.

## Galactic Gladiators

Gladiator

Warrior

Hero

Protector

Champion

Barbarian

Beast

Rogue

Guardian

Cyborg

Imperator

Hunter

Also Available as Audiobooks!

## PREVIEW: HELL SQUAD - MARCUS

**READY FOR ANOTHER?**

**IN THE AFTERMATH OF AN ALIEN INVASION:**

**HEROES WILL RISE...
WHEN THEY HAVE
SOMEONE TO LIVE FOR**

*In the aftermath of a deadly alien invasion, a band of survivors fights on...*

In a world gone to hell, Elle Milton—once the darling of the Sydney social scene—has carved a role for herself as the communications officer for the toughest commando team fighting for humanity's survival—Hell Squad. It's her chance to make a difference and make up for horrible past mistakes...despite the fact that its battle-hardened commander never wanted her on his team.

When Hell Squad is tasked with destroying a strategic alien facility, Elle knows they need her skills in the field. But first she must go head to head with Marcus Steele and convince him she won't be a liability.

Marcus Steele is a warrior through and through. He fights to protect the innocent and give the human race a chance to survive. And that includes the beautiful, gutsy Elle who twists him up inside with a single look. The last thing he wants is to take her into a warzone, but soon they are thrown together battling both the alien invaders and their overwhelming attraction. And Marcus will learn just how much he'll sacrifice to keep her safe.

### Hell Squad

Marcus

Cruz

Gabe

Reed

Roth

Noah

Shaw

Holmes

Niko

Finn

Theron

Hemi

Ash

Levi

Manu

Griff

Dom

Survivors

Tane

Also Available as Audiobooks!

**Team 52**

Mission: Her Protection

Mission: Her Rescue

Mission: Her Security

Mission: Her Defense

Mission: Her Safety

Mission: Her Freedom

Mission: Her Shield

Also Available as Audiobooks!

**Treasure Hunter Security**

Undiscovered

Uncharted

Unexplored

Unfathomed

Untraveled

Unmapped

Unidentified

Undetected

Also Available as Audiobooks!

**Eon Warriors**

Edge of Eon

Touch of Eon

Heart of Eon

Kiss of Eon

Mark of Eon

Also Available as Audiobooks!

## Galactic Gladiators: House of Rone

Sentinel

Defender

Centurion

Paladin

Guard

Also Available as Audiobooks!

## Galactic Gladiators

Gladiator

Warrior

Hero

Protector

Champion

Barbarian

Beast

Rogue

Guardian

Cyborg

Imperator

Hunter

Also Available as Audiobooks!

## Hell Squad

Marcus

Cruz

Gabe

Reed

Roth

Noah

Shaw

Holmes

Niko

Finn

Theron

Hemi

Ash

Levi

Manu

Griff

Dom

Survivors

Tane

Also Available as Audiobooks!

## The Anomaly Series

Time Thief

Mind Raider

Soul Stealer

Salvation

Anomaly Series Box Set

## The Phoenix Adventures

Among Galactic Ruins

At Star's End

In the Devil's Nebula

On a Rogue Planet

Beneath a Trojan Moon

Beyond Galaxy's Edge

On a Cyborg Planet

Return to Dark Earth

On a Barbarian World

Lost in Barbarian Space

Through Uncharted Space

Crashed on an Ice World

## Perma Series

Winter Fusion

A Galactic Holiday

**Warriors of the Wind**

Tempest

Storm & Seduction

Fury & Darkness

**Standalone Titles**

Savage Dragon

Hunter's Surrender

One Night with the Wolf

For more information visit www.annahackett.com

# ABOUT THE AUTHOR

I'm a USA Today bestselling romance author who's passionate about ***fast-paced, emotion-filled*** contemporary and science fiction romance. I love writing about people overcoming unbeatable odds and achieving seemingly impossible goals. I like to believe it's possible for all of us to do the same.

I live in Australia with my own personal hero and two very busy, always-on-the-move sons.

For release dates, behind-the-scenes info, free books, and other fun stuff, sign up for the latest news here:

Website: www.annahackett.com